A SECRET CONSEQUENCE FOR THE VISCOUNT

Sophia James

MILLS & BOON

Hidden among the back streets and cellars of an
underground Regency gentlemen's club, where
decadence, daring and debauchery abound,
the four owners of **Vitium et Virtus**
are about to meet their match!

Welcome to…

he Society of Wicked Gentlemen

Read

A Convenient Bride for the Soldier
by Christine Merrill

An Innocent Maid for the Duke
by Ann Lethbridge

A Pregnant Courtesan for the Rake
by Diane Gaston

A Secret Consequence for the Viscount
by Sophia James

All available now!

Author Note

I wrote the prologue for this book on a plane between Los Angeles and Melbourne after the Romance Writers of America® 2016 conference, and by the time I arrived home in Auckland I both understood and loved Nicholas Bartlett, the lost Viscount Bromley and one of the owners of the club Vitium et Virtus.

It was my absolute pleasure and privilege to work with Christine Merrill, Ann Lethbridge and Diane Gaston on The Society of Wicked Gentlemen series.

I hope you enjoy this last story, *A Secret Consequence for the Viscount*, as much as I enjoyed writing it.

Sophia James lives in Chelsea Bay, on Auckland, New Zealand's North Shore, with her husband who is an artist. She has a degree in English and History from Auckland University and believes her love of writing was formed by reading Georgette Heyer in the holidays at her grandmother's house. Sophia enjoys getting feedback at www.Facebook.com/sophiajamesauthor.

Books by Sophia James

Mills & Boon Historical Romance

Knight of Grace
Lady with the Devil's Scar
Gift-Wrapped Governesses
'Christmas at Blackhaven Castle'
Ruined by the Reckless Viscount

The Society of Wicked Gentlemen

A Secret Consequence for the Viscount

The Penniless Lords

Marriage Made in Money
Marriage Made in Shame
Marriage Made in Rebellion
Marriage Made in Hope

Men of Danger

Mistletoe Magic
Mistress at Midnight
Scars of Betrayal

The Wellingham Brothers

High Seas to High Society
One Unashamed Night
One Illicit Night
The Dissolute Duke

Visit the Author Profile page
at millsandboon.co.uk for more titles.

This book is dedicated to Linda Fildew,
my wonderful and irreplaceable editor,
who has been with me right from the start.
Thanks for knowing when to give me a push
to try new things.

Prologue

James River, Virginia—1818

He was bone-weary and cold and had been for a long time now.

He could feel it in his hands and heart and in the fury wrapped around each intake of breath, fear raw against the sound of the river.

Once he knew he had been different. Such knowledge sent a shaft of pain through him that was worse than anything else imaginable, an elusive certainty drifting on the edge of misunderstanding.

He swore as he lowered his body into the water, closing his eyes against the sting of cold. With the hand that still had feeling in it he grabbed at the rushes and steadied movement. He was here somewhere, the man who had slashed at him with a blade. He could feel his presence, close now, a shadow catching at space between darkness, barely visible. He held no weapon except for his wits, no way of protecting himself save for the years of desperation honed in distance. He couldn't remember ever feeling safe.

The voice came unexpectedly and close.

'Nicholas Bartlett? Are you there?'

The sound had him turning his head. For more or for less he knew not which. The name was familiar, its syllables distinct as they ran together into something that made a terrible and utter sense.

He wanted to stop the sudden onslaught of memories, each thread reforming itself into more, building a picture, words that pulled at the spinning void of his life and anchored him back into truth. A truth that lay above comprehension and disbelief.

More words came from the mouth of his stalker, moving before him, as he raised steel under a dull small moon.

'Vitium et Virtus.'

A prayer or a prophesy? A forecast of all that was to come or the harbinger of that which had been?

'No.' His own voice was suddenly certain as he shot out of the water to meet his fate, fury fuelling him. He hardly felt the slice of the knife against the soft bones of his face. He was fearless in his quest for life and as the curve of his assailant's neck came into his hands he understood a primal power that did away with doubt and gave him back hope. He felt the small breakage of bone and saw surprise in the dark bulging eyeballs under moonlight. The hot breath on the raised skin of his own forearm slowed and cooled as resistance changed into flaccidity. Life lost into death with barely a noise save the splash of a corpse as it was taken by the wide flowing James to sink under the blackness, a moment's disturbance and then calm, the small ridges slipping into the former patterns of the river.

He sat down on the bank in the wet grass and placed his head between his knees, both temples aching with the movement.

Vitium et Virtus.

Nicholas Bartlett.

He knew the words, knew this life, knew the name imbued into each and every part of him.

Nicholas Henry Stewart Bartlett.

Viscount Bromley.

A crest with a dragon on the dexter side and a horse on the sinister. Both in argent.

An estate in Essex.

Oliver. Frederick. Jacob.

The club of secrets.

Vitium et Virtus.

'Hell.' It all came tumbling back without any barriers. Flashes of honour, shame, disorder and excess after so very many years of nothing.

Tears welled, mixed with blood as the loss of who he now was melded against the sorrow of everything forgotten.

The young and dissolute London Lord with the world at his feet and a thousand hours of leisure and ease before him had been replaced by this person he had become, a life formed by years of endurance and hardship.

'Nicholas Bartlett.'

He turned the name on his tongue and said it quietly into the night so he might hear it truly. The tinge of the Americas stretched long over the vowels in a cadence at odds with his English roots, though when he repeated it again he heard only the sorrow.

He searched back to the last memories held of that time, but could just think of being at Bromworth Manor in Essex with his uncle.

Arguing yet again. After that there was nothing. He could not remember returning to London or getting on a ship to the Americas. He recalled pain somewhere and the vague sense of water. Perhaps he had been picked up by a boat, a stranger without memory and shanghaied aboard?

He knew he would not have disappeared willingly though his gambling debts had been rising as he had been drawn into the seedy halls of London where cheating was rife. There had been threats to pay up or else, but he had by and large managed to do so. His friends had been there to help him through the worst of the demands and he also had the club in Mayfair. A home. A family. A place that felt like his. He loved Jacob Huntingdon, Frederick Challenger and Oliver Gregory like the brothers he'd never had.

Shaking fingers touched the ache on his cheek near his right eye and came away with the sticky redness of oozing blood.

The eye felt strange and unfocused. The night was so dark he wondered if he had gone blind in that eye, a last gift from his pursuer. He shut the other one and tried to find an image, holding his fingers up against what little light there was on the water, and was relieved to see a blurry outline.

He did not feel up to walking back yet through the reeds and the river path to the shade of the cottonwoods. He didn't want others to see him like this and he needed to make certain there were not more who would be trying to hurt him. A tiredness swept over everything, a grief at the loss of a life at his own hands. He had not killed before and the quickness of fear was now replaced by an ennui of guilt.

How could he ever fit in again? How could he be the lord he was supposed to be after this? Had his assailant held a family close? Had he been only doing a job he was sent to complete? The grey shadows in which he'd lived the last six years were things familiar. The sludgy silhouette of them, the blacks and whites of shining morality left as other men's choices but not available to him. Twice before in America others had tried to kill him; different men in the pay of a shadowy enemy and the mastermind at pulling the strings.

He had used so many different names as he moved on for ever, away from discovery, fleeing relationships. In the end he only brought people harm and danger. If they got to know him they were always at risk and so he had not allowed such closeness. Twice before he had felt his stalkers near.

Emily. The young daughter of the kindly reverend and his wife who had taken him in had been pushed off a cliff top. The girl had survived by clinging to the undergrowth, but he had understood that after that for him there could never be intimacy with anyone.

New towns, different jobs and a series of women with favours for sale had followed. He did not seek out decent company again, but dwelt in the underworld of secrets, squalor and shallow rapport. He understood the people who were as brutalised and damaged as himself and there was safety in the shifting unsettled disconnection of outsiders.

Peter Kingston. His name now here in the river town of Richmond, the capital of the Colony and Dominion of Virginia. He could disappear tomorrow and nobody would miss him, the man employed at the tavern of Shockoe Bottom who seldom spoke and hardly ever smiled. Stranger. Foreigner. Outsider. Murderer now. Another name added to all the ones he had gathered. A further disengagement. A shadow who had walked through the Americas with barely a footprint. Until to-night. Until now. Until his hands had fastened around the throat of his pursuer and broken the life from him.

He leant over and was neatly sick into the green heart of some poison ivy.

Leaves of three, let them be.

The ditty came of its own accord as he wiped his mouth with the frayed edge of his jacket. Had he been truly regretful he might have laid his hand across the plant and allowed its penance. As it was he merely frowned at such an idea and stood.

He would gather his few possessions and find a ship to England. Frederick, Oliver and Jacob would help him to make sense of things and then he would leave London to retire to the country in Essex. Alone. It was the only way he could see before him.

As he looked back a fog bank slid by on the flat black current of the James.

Chapter One

∾∾∾

It was one day past Christmas.

That thought made Nicolas smile. He had forgotten the celebration for so long in the Americas that the presence of it here in London was somehow comforting. A continued and familiar tradition, a belief that transcended all difficulty and promised hope for the likes of himself? Or would it tender despair? He could not imagine any church exonerating his sins should he be foolish enough to confess them.

The age-old music of carols could be heard as he left the narrow service alley behind the club of Vitium et Virtus in Mayfair and came around to the front door. Here the only sound was that of laughter and frivolity, a card game underway, he guessed, in the downstairs salon. High stakes and well funded. The few coins he had left in his own pocket felt paltry and he wondered for the millionth time whether he should have come at all.

The late afternoon lengthened the shadows. He could slip away still, undetected, and make his way north. Boxing Day kept most people at home enjoying the company of family. There would be few around to note his progress.

He swallowed as he looked up and saw the sky was stained in red. Blood red. Guilt red. A celestial nod to his culpability or a pardon written in colour?

Digging into his pocket, he found a silver shilling.

'Heads I stay and tails I go.' It was all he could think of at this moment, a choice that was arbitrary and random. The coin turned and as it came down into his opened palm the face of George the Third was easily visible. The thought crossed his mind that had it been tails he would have tried for the best of three.

His knuckles were against the main door before he knew it, the polished black lacquer of the portal attesting to great care and attention and a certain understated wealth.

When it opened a big man he did not know

stood there, dressed in the clothes of a footman, but with the visage of one who knew his intrinsic worth.

'Can I help you, sir?'

Nicholas could feel the condescension. His clothes from the long voyage were dirty and they had not been well looked after. His beard was full and his hair uncut. He was glad there was no looking glass inside the door to reflect his image over and over again.

'Are any of the lords who own this place present inside this evening?'

He tried to round his vowels and sound at least halfway convincing. It would not take much for the man to bid those who guarded the front door to throw him out. He knew there was desperation in his eyes.

'They are, sir.'

'Could you show me through to them?'

'Indeed, sir. But may I take your hat and coat first and could you give me your name?'

'Bromley. They will know me.'

'If you would just wait here, sir.' The footman snagged Nick's attire across a series of wooden pegs carved into the shape of a man's sexual parts inside the front door. The sheer overtness of the furnishings shocked him now, where once it had not.

A further confusion. Another way in which he had changed. He swallowed and as dryness filled his mouth he wished he'd thought to bring his brandy flask.

Then there was the sound of chairs scraping against the floor and the rush of feet, a door flung back against its hinges and three faces he knew like his own before him. Astonished. Disbelieving.

'Nicholas?' It was Jacob who came forward first just as he knew it would be. Rakish and handsome, there had always been an undercurrent of kindness within him, a care for the underdog, a certainty of faith.

Oliver and Frederick followed him, each one as bewildered as the next.

'You've been gone for more than six damn years…' It was Oliver who said this, the flush of emotion visible across the light brown of his skin.

'And to turn up like this without any correspondence? Why would you not let us know where you were or how you fared at least?' Fred's voice cracked as his glance took in Nick's cheek and the bandage on his left hand holding the deep wound safe from further damage.

Twenty-five days at sea had not helped the

healing. It ached so much he had taken to cradling it across his body, easing the pain and heat. He released it now and let it hang at his side, taking hope from the bare emotion of his friends even as his fingers throbbed in protest.

'Thank the Lord you are returned.' Oliver stepped towards him and wrapped his arms around all the damaged parts of his body. It had been such a very long time since someone had touched him like this that he stiffened. Then Fred was there and Jake, enveloping him so tight in an embrace he hardly knew where one of them stopped and another one started.

Safety. For the first time in years Nicholas took a breath that was not forced. Yet despite this, he himself reached out to none of them. Not yet. Not till it was over. Protecting each of them from harm was the only thing he now had left to offer.

He should not have come. He should not have been so selfish. He should have listened to his inner voice and stayed away until he knew where the danger had come from. But friendship held its own beacons and the hope of it had led him here, hurrying across the seas.

'This unexpected reunion calls for a celebration.' Fred spoke as he hauled Nicholas back into the private drawing room at the end of the corridor, the others following. A table set up for poker had been dismantled in the rush of their exit, the cards fallen and the chips scattered. Just that fact warmed him and when Oliver chose an unopened bottle from a cabinet in the corner and poured them each a drink, Nick took it gratefully.

He waited till the others filled their glasses and raised his own.

'To friendship,' he said simply.

'To the future,' Jake added.

'May the truth of what has happened to you, Nicholas, hold us together,' Fred's words were serious and when Oliver smiled the warmth in his green eyes was overlaid by question.

The cognac was smooth, creamy and strong and unlike any home-brewed liquor Nick had become so adept at dispensing in the cheap bars of the east coast of the Americas. The kick in it took his breath away. The flavour of his youth, he thought, unappreciated and im-bibed in copious amounts. Today he savoured it and let it slide off the back of his tongue.

When Jacob motioned to the others to sit Nick took his place at the head of the table. This was where he had always sat, his initials carved into the dark mahogany of the chair. The first finger of his right hand ran across the marking, the ridges beneath tracing his past.

'We never erased anything of you, Nicholas. We always believed that you would be back. But why so long? Why leave it for so many years before returning?' Jacob voiced just what he imagined the others were thinking.

'I had amnesia. I could not remember who I was or where I had been. My memory only began to function again in the Americas five weeks ago after encountering a man who wanted me dead.'

'He nearly succeeded by the looks of it.'

'Nearly, but not quite. He came off worse.'

'You killed him.' The soldier in Fred asked this question and there was no room in his answer for lies.

'I did.'

'We found blood in the alley behind Vitium et Virtus the morning after you disappeared.' Jacob stood at that and walked over to the mantel to dig into a gilded box. 'This was found, too.'

His signet ring surprised him. He had always worn it, but had forgotten that he had.

The burnished gold crest caught at the light above. *Servire Populo.* To serve the people. The irony in such a motto had been humorous to him once given his youthful overarching ability to only serve himself. Reaching out, he took the piece between his fingers, wincing at the dirt under his nails and the scars across his knuckles. He swallowed back the lump that was growing in his throat.

His old life offered back with such an easy grace.

'I can't remember what happened in the alley.'

'What was the last thing you remember then? Before you disappeared?'

'Arguing at Bromworth Manor with my uncle. It was hot and I was damnably drunk. It was my birthday, the fifteenth of August.'

'You disappeared the next Saturday night then, a week later. That much at least we have established.' Fred gave this information.

'Did you know that your uncle has taken over the use of the Bromley title?' Oliver leant back against the leather in his chair and raised his feet up on an engraved ottoman, his stance belying the tension in his voice. 'He wants you declared dead legally, given the number of years you have been missing. He has begun the procedure.'

'The bastard has the temerity to call himself your protector,' Jacob snarled, 'when all he wants is your inheritance and your estates.'

Nicholas took in the information with numbed indifference. Aaron Bartlett had never been easy but, as his late father's only brother, he'd had the credentials to take over the guardianship of an eight-year-old orphan. Nicholas remembered the day his uncle had walked into Bromworth Manor a week after his parents' death, both avarice and greed in his eyes.

'He's a charlatan and everyone knows it and I for one would love to be there when you throw him lock, stock and barrel out of your ancestral home.' As Oliver said this the others nodded. 'Do you think he had any part in your disappearance?'

Nicholas had wondered this himself, but without memory or proof he had no basis on which to found an opinion. Shrugging his shoulders, he finished the last of his cognac and was pleased when Jacob refilled the glass again.

He held the signet ring tight in his right hand, a small token of who he was and of what he had been. He did not want to place it on his finger again just yet because the wearing of it implied a different role and one he didn't feel up to trying to fill. He had walked under many names in the Americas, but the shadow of his persona here was as foreign to him now as those other identities he had adopted.

Jacob and Fred each wore a wedding ring. That thought shocked him out of complacency and for the first time he asked his own question.

'You are married?'

The smiles were broad and genuine, but it was Jacob who answered first.

'You have been gone a long time, Nicholas, and dissoluteness takes some effort in maintaining. There comes a day when you look elsewhere for real happiness and each of us has found that. Oliver may well be wed soon, too.'

'Then I am glad for it.'

And he was, he thought with relief. He was pleased for their newfound families, pleased that they had managed to move forward even if he had not. 'Can I meet them? Your women?'

'Tomorrow night.' Fred said. 'We have a

function at my town house with all the trimmings and a guest list of about eighty. You look as though you could do with a careful introduction, Nick, and such a number would not be too daunting for a first foray back into English society.'

'You will need the services of a barber and a physician before others see you. Fred is about your size so with a tailor to iron out the differences you could get away with wearing his clothes.' Jacob watched him carefully, his blue eyes sharp on detail. When his glance ran over his face Nick knew he would have to say something, his good hand going up to the ruined cheek as though he might hide it a little.

'If someone still wishes me dead, perhaps it would be better not to involve any of you in this. I should not want…'

Fred shook his head. 'We are involved already as your friends. There is no way you could stop any of us helping you.'

Oliver placed his hand on the table palm up in the way they had since their very first meeting and the others laid theirs on top. It took only a second's hesitation before he found his own above theirs joined in the flesh and in promise.

'In Vitium et Virtus.' They all said the words together. In *Vice and Virtue*. The motto seemed more appropriate at this second than it ever had before.

'We should retire to my town house for a drink. There is more of this cognac there and the occasion calls for further celebration. You can stay with me for as long as you need to, Nick, for I will have a room readied for you.'

Jacob's invitation was tempting. 'The offer is a kind one, but I'm reluctant to place you in danger.' He needed to say this to allow Jacob the chance of refusal at least.

'I think I can take care of myself and my family. Let's just worry about getting to the bottom of this mystery, to help you recover the final bits of memory you seem to have lost. If you can start to remember the faces of your assailants in the alley that may lead us to the perpetrator.'

'How does amnesia work, anyway?' Oliver asked this question and Fred answered.

'In the army many people lost their memories for the short term. A day or two at the most due to trauma, though I knew of a few chaps who never recovered theirs at all.'

'I don't think Nick wants to hear about those ones, Fred.' When Jacob said this they all laughed. 'At least he remembers us and the club.'

'It would be hard to forget.' Nicholas gestured to the excess and the luxury. 'But it is the friendships I recall the most.' His voice cracked on the last words and he swallowed away the emotion. He was not here for pity or sympathy. He knew he looked half the man who had left England, with his filthiness and his wounds but it was the hidden hurts that worried him the most. Could he ever trust anyone again? Was he doomed for ever to hold himself apart from others, all the shadows within him cutting him off from true intimacy?

He could see in each of his friends' eyes that they found him altered, more brittle. But the lord who had cared not a whit for social convention was long gone, too, that youth of reckless pleasure seeking debauchery and high-stakes gambling. If he met a younger version of himself now he doubted he would even like him very much.

The uncertainty in him built. He did not respect his past nor his present and his future looked less rosy than he imagined it might have on returning to England. Each of his friends had a woman now, a family, a place to live and be. His own loneliness felt more acute given the pathway they had taken. He had missed his direction and even the thought of confronting his guardian in the large and dusty halls of Bromworth Manor had become less appealing than it had been on the boat over.

Did he want it all back, the responsibility and the problems? Did he need to be a viscount? Such a title would confine him once again to society ways and manners, things which now seemed pointless and absurd.

Even the club had lost its sheen, the dubious morality of vice and pleasure outdated and petty. The overt sexuality disturbed him. From where he sat he could see a dozen or more statues of women in various stages of undress and sensual arousal. The paintings of couplings on the wall were more brazen than he could ever remember, more distasteful.

In America he had seen the effects of prostitution on boys, girls and women in a way he had never noticed here, the thrill of the fantasy and daring dimmed under the reality. For every coin spent to purchase a dream for someone there was a nightmare hidden beneath for another.

'You seem quiet, Nicholas? Are you well?'

Jacob had leant over to touch his arm and the unexpected contact made him jump and pull away. He knew they had all noticed such a reaction and struggled to hide his fury.

Everything was wrong. He was wrong to come and expect it all to have been just as it was. The headache he had been afflicted with ever since his recovery of memory chose that moment to develop into a migraine, his sight jumping between the faces of his friends and cutting them into small jagged prisms of distortion.

He wished he could just lie down here on the floor on an Aubusson rug that was thick and clean and close his eyes. He wished for darkness and silence. He hated himself as he began to shake violently and was thankful when Oliver crossed the room having found a woollen blanket, tucking it in gently around his shoulders.

Chapter Two

Lady Eleanor Huntingdon kissed her five-year-old sleeping daughter on the forehead before tiptoeing out of the bedroom.

Lucy was the very centre of her life, the shining star of a love and happiness that she had never expected to find again after…

'No'. She said the word firmly. She would not think of *him*. Not tonight when her world was soft and warm and she had a new book on the flowers of England to read from Lackington's. Tonight she would simply relax and enjoy.

Her brother Jacob was downstairs chatting to someone in his library and Rose, his wife, had retired a good half an hour ago, pleading exhaustion after a particularly frantic day.

Her own day had been busy, too, with all the celebrations, guilt and sorrow eating into her reserves as yet another Christmas went by without any sign of Lucy's father.

'No.' She said it again this time even more firmly. She would not dwell on the past for the next few hours because the despair and wretchedness of the memory always left her with a headache. Tonight she would dream of him, she knew she would, for his face was reflected in the shape of her daughter's and this evening the resemblance had been even more apparent than usual.

She sat on the damask sofa in the small salon attached to her room and opened her book. She had already poured herself a glass of wine and had a slice of the apple pie the cook had made that night for dinner beside it. Everything she needed right there. Outside it was cold, the first snows of winter on the ground. Inside a fire roared in the hearth, the sound of it comforting.

She seldom came to the city, but she had journeyed down to be with her family in the autumn and had decided to stay for the Christmas celebrations, the food and the decorations—things that Lucy needed in her life. She would leave tomorrow with her daughter for Millbrook House, the ancestral estate of the Westmoor dukedom in Middlesex. Her home now. The place she loved the most in all the world.

Opening her book, she began to read about the new varieties of roses, a plant she enjoyed and grew there in the sheltered courtyard gardens. She could hear her brother's voice from the downstairs library more distinctly now. He must have opened the door that led into the passageway and his quiet burr filled the distance.

She stopped reading and looked up, tilting her head against the silence. The other voice sounded vaguely familiar, but she could not quite place its tone. It was not Frederick Challenger or Oliver Gregory, she knew that, but there was a familiarity there that was surprising. The click of a door shutting banished any sound back into the faraway distance, but still she felt anxious.

She was missing something. Something important. Placing the book on her small table, she stood and picked up the glass of wine, walking to the window and pulling back the curtains to look out over the roadway.

No stranger's carriage stood before the house so perhaps the newcomer had come home in her brother's conveyance from Mayfair, for she knew Jacob had been to his club.

Her eyes strayed to the clock. It was well after ten. Still early enough in London terms for an outing, but late for a private visitor on a cold and rainy evening. She stopped herself from instructing her maid to go down and enquire as to the name of the caller. This hesitancy also worried her for usually she would have no such qualms in doing such a thing.

A tremor of concern passed through her body, making her hands shake. She was twenty-four years old and the last six difficult years had fashioned such strength and independence that she now had no time for the timidity she was consumed with. If she was worried she needed to go downstairs herself and understand just where her anxieties lay.

But still she did not move as she finished her wine in a long and single swallow and poured herself another.

There was danger afoot for both herself and Lucy.

That horrible thought made her swear out loud, something she most rarely did. Cursing again under her breath, she took a decent swallow of the next glass of wine and then placed it on the mantel. The fire beneath burnt hot. She could see the red sparks of flame against the back of the chimney flaring into life and then dying out.

Soldiers.

Ralph, Jacob and herself had played games in winter with them for all the young years of their life. Her hand went to her mouth to try to contain the grief her oldest brother's death had left her with. With reverence she recited the same prayer she always did when she thought of him.

'And the dead in Christ will rise first. Then we who are alive, who are left, will be caught up together with them in the clouds...'

It was a snippet from one of the verses of Thessalonians, but the image of her and her brothers rising whole into the sky was a lovely one. Lucy would be there, of course, and Rose and Grandmama, as well, and all the other people that she loved.

She was not particularly religious, but she did believe in something—in God, she supposed, and Jesus and the Holy Family with their goodness. How else could she have got through her trials otherwise?

She was sick of her thoughts tonight, fed up with their constant return to *him*.

That damn voice was still there in her mind, too, changing itself into the tones of the man she had loved above all else and then lost.

The hidden name. The unuttered father. Although she knew Jacob suspected she had told their father, she had never told anyone at all exactly what had happened to her, because sometimes she could barely understand it herself.

For a moment she breathed in deeply to try to stop the tears that were pooling in her eyes. She would not cry, not tonight with a fire, a good book, some apple pie and French wine.

Her life had taken on some sort of pattern that felt right and she loved her daughter with all her heart.

The door downstairs was ajar again and the voices came more clearly than they had before. Her brother sounded perturbed, angry even, and she stood still to listen, opening her own door so that the words would be formed with more precision.

'You cannot possibly think that we will not help you. All of us. There is no damn way in the world that I will let you go and fight this by yourself.'

'But it is dangerous, Jake. If anything were to happen to you and your family...'

The room began to spin around Eleanor, in

a terrifying and dizzying spiral. There was no up and down, only the vortex of a weightless imbalance pulling at her throat and her heart and her soul.

Nicholas Bartlett. It was his voice, lost for all these years. To her and to Lucy. To Jacob and Frederick and Oliver. Why was he down there?

He had not come to see her? He had not beaten down her door in the rush of reunion? He had not called her name from the bottom of the stairs again and again as he had stormed up to find her before taking her into his arms and kissing her as he had done once? Relentlessly. Passionately. Without thought for anyone or anything.

He had sat with her brother discussing his own needs for all the evening. Quietly. Civilly.

Perhaps he did not know she was here, but even that implied a lack of enquiring on his behalf. The man she remembered would have asked her brother immediately as to her whereabouts and moved heaven and earth to find her.

She nodded her head in order to underline such a truth.

Her own heart was beating so fast and

strong she could see the motion of it beneath the thick woollen bodice of her blue-wool gown. Eleanor wondered if she might simply perish with the shock of it before she ever saw him.

Sitting down, she took a deep breath, placing her head in her hands and closing her eyes.

She needed to calm herself. This was the moment she had dreamed about for years and years and it was not supposed to be anything like this. She should be running down the stairs calling his name, joy in her voice and delight in her eyes.

Instead she stood and found her white wrap to wind it tightly about her shoulders because, whether she wanted to admit it or not, there had been a hesitancy and a withdrawal between them on the last night they had been together.

He'd seen her off, of course, in his carriage, but he had not acted then like a man who was desperate for her company.

'Thank you, Eleanor.' He had said that as he'd moved back and away from the kiss she had tried to give him, as if relieved for the space, his glance sliding to the ground.

He had not even stayed to watch her as the

conveyance had departed, the emptiness reflected in her own feelings of dread.

So now, here, six years later she could not quite fathom where such an absence left her. What if she went downstairs now and saw this thought exactly on his face? Would her heart break again? Could she even withstand it?

She had to see him. She had to find in his velvet-brown eyes the truth between them. There was a mistake, a misunderstanding, a wrongness she could not quite identify.

Her feet were on the stairs before she knew it, hurrying down. A short corridor and then the library, the door closed against her. Without hesitation she pushed the portal open and strode through.

Nicholas Bartlett, Viscount Bromley, was sitting on the wing chair by the fire and he looked nothing like how she remembered him.

His clothes were dirty, his hair unshaped, but it was the long curling scar that ran from one corner of his eye almost to his mouth that she saw first.

Ruined.

His beautiful handsome face had been sliced in half.

'Eleanor.' Her brother had risen and there

was delight in his expression. 'Nicholas has been returned to us safely from all his years abroad in the Americas. He will be staying here at our town house for a time.'

'The Americas…?' She could only stand and stare, for although Nicholas Bartlett had also risen he made no effort at all to cross the floor to greet her. Rather he stood there with his brandy held by a hand that was dressed with a dirty bandage and merely tipped his head.

In formal acknowledgement. Like a stranger might do or an acquaintance. His cheeks were flushed, the eyes so much harder than she remembered them being and his countenance brittle somehow, all sureness gone.

For a second she could not quite think what to say.

'It has been a long time.' Foolish words. Words that might be construed as hanging her heart on her sleeve?

He nodded and the thought of his extreme weariness hit her next. Lifting her hand to her heart, she stayed quiet.

'Six years,' he returned as if she had not been counting, as though he needed to give her the time precisely because the duration had been lost in the interim.

Six years, seventeen weeks and six days. She knew the time almost to the very second.

'Indeed, my lord.' She swallowed then and saw her brother looking at her, puzzlement across his face, for the hard anger in her voice had been distinct.

'You welcome my best friend back only with distant words, Eleanor, when you seemed most distraught at his disappearance?'

God, she would have to touch him. She would have to put her arms around his body and pretend he was nothing and nobody. Just her brother's friend. The very thought of that made her swallow.

He had not moved at all from his place by the fire and he had not put his glass down either. Stay away, such actions said. Stay on your side of the room and I shall stay on mine.

'I am glad to see you, Lord Bromley. I am glad that you are safe and well.'

His smile floored her, the deep dimple in his un-ruined cheek so very known.

'Thank you, Lady Eleanor.' He held up his injured hand. 'Altered somewhat, but still alive.'

The manner of his address made her sway and she might have fallen had she not steadied herself on the back rest of the nearby sofa.

His dark brown hair was lank and loose, the sheen she remembered there gone.

'I heard you had been married to a lord in Scotland and now have a child. Your brother spoke of it. How old is your daughter?'

Terror reached out and gripped her, winding its claws into the danger of an answer.

Without hesitation she moved slightly and knocked her brother's full glass of red wine from the table upon which it sat. The liquid spilled on to the cream carpet beneath, staining the wool like blood. The glass shattered into a thousand splinters as it bounced further against the parquet flooring.

Such an action broke all thought of answering Nicholas Bartlett's question as her brother leapt forward.

'Ellie, stay back or you will cut yourself.'

Ellie? The name seared into some part of Nicholas's mind like a living flame. He knew this name well, but how could that be?

He shook his head and looked away. He knew Jacob's sister only slightly. She had been so much younger than her brother when he was here last, a green girl recently introduced into society. But she had always been attractive.

Now she was a beauty, her dark hair pulled back in a style so severe it only enhanced the shape of her face and the vivid blueness of her eyes. Eyes that cut through him in a bruised anger. He knew she had spilt the wine on purpose for he had spent enough years with duplicity to know the difference between intention and accident.

He'd asked of the age of her daughter? Was there something wrong with the child, some problem that made the answer untenable to her?

Jacob looked as puzzled as he probably did, the wine soaking into his carpet with all the appearance of never being able to be removed.

A permanent stain.

He saw Eleanor had sliced her finger in her attempt at retrieving the long stem of crystal that had once been attached to the shattered bowl. He wished she had left it for the maid who was now bustling around her feet sweeping the fragments into a metal holder.

'I need to go and see to my hand.' Eleanor's words came with a breathless relief, the red trail of blood sliding down her middle finger as she held it in the air. 'Please excuse me.'

She looked at neither of them as she scurried away.

When she was gone and the maid had departed, too, Jacob's frown deepened. 'Eleanor has been sad since the death of her husband. Widowhood weighs heavily upon her.'

'How did her husband die?'

'Badly.' The same flush of complicity he had seen on his sister's visage covered Jacob's face.

Since he had been gone the Huntingdon family had suffered many tragedies. Jacob had told him of the loss of Ralph, the oldest brother and heir, and his father in a carriage accident. In the telling of it Nicholas had gained the distinct impression that Jacob blamed himself somehow for their loss.

His friends had their demons, too. That thought softened his own sense of dislocation. The hedonistic decadence of the club had not been all encompassing. Real life had a way of grabbing one by the throat and strangling the air out of hope. Perhaps no one reached their thirties without some sort of a loss? A rite of passage, a way of growth? A bitter truth of life?

He wished Eleanor Huntingdon might have stayed and talked longer. He wished she might have come forward and welcomed him back in the way her brother had directed. With touch.

* * *

She reached her room and threw herself upon her bed, face buried in her pillow as she screamed out her grief. Six years of sorrow and loss and hope and love. For nothing.

Six years of waiting for the moment Nicholas Bartlett might return with all sorts of plausible explanations as to why he'd been away for so very long and how he had fought hard to be back at her side again, his heart laid at her feet.

The truth of tonight had a sharper edge altogether. Was he just another rake who had simply made a conquest of a young girl with foolishness in her heart? She had offered him exactly what it was he sought—the use of her body for a heady sensual interlude, a brief flirtation that had meant the world to her. Had it meant nothing at all to him?

'I. Hate. Him.'

He had looked at her like a stranger might, no inkling as to what had passed between them in his bedroom at the Bromley town house, when he had whispered things into her ear that made her turn naked into the warmth of him and allow him everything.

Swallowing hard, she thought she might be sick.

Lucy might never have the promise of a father now, a papa who would fold her in his arms and tell her she meant the world to him and that he would always protect her.

The family she'd imagined to have for years was gone, burst in the bubble of just one look from his velvet-brown eyes and his complete indifference. And the worst thing of all was that she would have to see him again and again both here in the house and at any social occasion because he was her only brother's best friend.

That thought had her sitting and swiping angrily at her eyes.

She would not waste her tears. She would confront him and tell him that to her it was as if he was dead and that she wished for no more discourse between them.

Then she would leave London for Millbrook and stay there till the hurt began to soften and the fury loosened its hold.

She would survive this. She had to for Lucy's sake. She had seen other women made foolish by the loss of love and dreams and simply throw their lives away. But not her. She was strong and resolute.

Taking in a shaky breath, she walked over to her writing desk and drew out paper. She would ask to meet him tonight in the summer house in the garden, a place they had met once before in their few heady days of courtship.

She would not be kind and filter out any of the 'what had been'. She would throw his disloyalty in his face and make him understand that such a betrayal was as loathsome to her as it was hurtful. No. Not that word. She did not wish for Nicholas Bartlett, Viscount Bromley, to know in any way that he had entirely broken her heart.

Chapter Three

He was exhausted. His migraine had dulled to a constant headache and all he wanted to do was to sleep.

Tomorrow he would clean himself up. He would have his hair cut, his beard shaved and find some clothes that were not torn and dirty. He would also see a doctor about his hand because it felt hot and throbbing and he was sure an inflammation had set in. But for now... sleep, and the bed in the chamber Jacob had given him on the second floor looked large and inviting.

A sheet of paper placed carefully on the pillow caught his attention and he walked across to lift it up.

Meet me at the summer house as the clock strikes one. It is important.
Eleanor Huntingdon

Surprise floored him. Why would she send him this? Even his own dubious moral code knew the danger in such a meeting.

Her writing was precise and evenly sloped, and she had not used her married surname. He could smell a perfume on the paper that made him bring the sheet to his nose and breath in. Violets.

A mantel clock above the fireplace told him it was already fifteen minutes before the hour she had stated. Pulling his coat from the one bag he had brought as luggage from the Americas, he let himself quietly out of the room.

Ten minutes later he saw her coming through the drifts of dirty snow, a small figure wrapped in a thick shawl that fell almost to her knees. The moon was out and the wind had dropped and in the silence all about it was as if they were the only two people left in the world.

Her face was flushed from cold as she came in, shutting the glass door behind her. In here the chill was lessened, whether from the abundance of green plant life or just good building practice, he knew not which. When she spoke though he could see a cloud of mist after each word.

'Thank you for coming.'

'You thought I would not?'

She ignored that and rushed on. 'I was more than surprised to see you tonight. I don't know why you would wish for all those years of silence and no contact whatsoever, but—'

'It was not intentional, Lady Eleanor. My memory was lost.'

Her eyes widened at this truth and she swallowed, hard.

'I must have been hit over the head, as there was a sizeable lump there for a good time afterwards. As a result of the injury my memory was compromised.'

She now looked plainly shocked. 'How much of it exactly? How much did you lose?'

'Everything that happened to me before I disappeared was gone for many years. A month ago I retrieved most of my history but still…there are patches.'

'Patches?'

'The week before my disappearance and a few days after have gone entirely. I cannot seem to remember any of it.'

She turned at that, away from the moonlight so that all her face was in shadow. She seemed slighter than she had done a few hours earlier. Her hands trembled as she caught them together before her.

'Everything?'

'I am hoping it will come back, but…' He stopped, because he could not know if this was a permanent state or a temporary one.

'How was your cheek scarred?'

'Someone wants me dead. They have tried three times to kill me now and I doubt that will cease until I identify the perpetrators.'

'Why? Why should you be such a target?'

'I have lived in the shadows for a long time, even before I left England, and have any number of enemies. Some I can identify, but others I can't.'

'A lonely place to be in.'

'And a dangerous one.'

'You are different now, Lord Bromley.' She gave him those words quietly. 'More distant. A harder man. Almost unrecognisable.'

He laughed, the sound discordant, but here in the night there was a sense of honesty he had not felt in a long, long time. Even his friends had tiptoed around his new reality and tried to find the similarities with what had been before. Lady Eleanor did not attempt to be diplomatic at all as she had asked of his cheek and his circumstances and there was freedom in such truth.

He felt a pull towards her that was stronger than anything he had ever known before and stiffened, cursing beneath his breath. She was Jacob's younger sister and he could offer her nothing. He needed to be careful.

'I am less whole, I think.' His good hand gestured at his face. 'Less trusting.'

'Like me,' she returned in a whisper. 'Just the same.'

And when her blue eyes met his, he saw the tears that streamed down her cheeks, sorrow, anger and grief written all over her face.

He touched her then. He took her hand into his own to try to give the coldness some warmth. A small hand with bitten-down nails. There was a ring on the third finger, encrusted diamonds in gold.

'Was he a good man, your husband?'

'I thought so.'

'Then I am sorry for it.'

At that she snatched her fingers from his grasp and turned. She was gone before he could say another word, a shadow against the hedgerows, small and alone.

Why had she asked him here? What had she said that could not have been discussed in the breakfast salon in the morning? Why had she risked such a meeting in the very dead of night just to ask of his health?

Nothing made any sense.

Everything was now dangerous.

Nicholas being here, the desperate people who were chasing him, the new man he had become at the expense of the one he had been.

She barely recognised him inside or out. He looked different and he sounded different. Bigger. More menacing. Distant. And yet… when he had taken her hand into his she had felt the giddy rush of want and desire.

'Nicholas.' She whispered his name into the night as she sat by the fire.

'Amnesia.' She breathed the word quietly, hating the sound of it.

Lucy had been her priority for all the years of their apartness. She had risked her social standing, her family's acceptance and her future for her daughter and if there was even a slight chance that Nicholas could place her in danger then Eleanor was not prepared to take it.

He had said the perpetrators had attacked him three times already and had looked as though he expected a fourth or a fifth or a sixth. What was it she had heard him say to her brother just a few hours ago as she had over-listened to their conversation in the library?

'But it is dangerous, Jake. If anything were to happen to you or your family...'

If she told him the truth about that week before he disappeared, would he want to be back in their lives? Did she want to risk telling him of their closeness, knowing so little about him? He was a stranger to her now, so perhaps she should wait to discover what kind of man he was before revealing a secret so huge it would change all their lives for ever.

These thoughts tumbled around and around in her mind, going this way and that. If he had just looked at her for a second as he used to, she knew she would have capitulated and let him know everything. But this new Nicholas was altered and aloof, the indifference in his eyes crushing.

Lucy was now her priority. As a mother she needed to make decisions that would protect her child. She had not told another soul about her relationship with Nicholas. Jacob had been distraught from the loss of his friend and she thought he might not cope with another heartbreak and scandal. She had never seen her brother so broken.

And so she had told her family nothing of the father and lover and instead, with their help, had removed to Scotland and away from prying eyes.

Goodness, those years had been hard, she thought, and shook her head. She had been so lonely she might have simply died, there in Edinburgh in the house Jacob had set her up in waiting until she could return to Millbrook for the birth of her child. A terrible secret, a dreadful scandal and all the hope of what could have been disappeared as completely as Nicholas Bartlett had.

Blighted by her own stupidity, she'd lived in sadness until the first look at the face of her daughter had banished any regret.

On her return she found Jacob had concocted a story of a husband who had died and that she was now a grieving young widow with a small child in tow. She had become Eleanor Robertson at the stroke of a pen, the name being a common and unremarkable one, though she never thought of herself as such and used Huntingdon when signing letters to anyone she knew well. Oh, granted, she realised that many people did not believe such a fabrication, but nobody made a fuss of it either. She was a duke's daughter with land and money of her own and in the very few times she'd returned to the city she found the few friends she still did have to be generally accepting of her circumstances.

A fragile existence that only took the renewed appearance of Nicholas Bartlett to break it down completely. But this missing week seemed well established in his mind and he himself had said it had been a month since any recall had returned.

Which meant no other memories had crept back in. She did not know enough about the state of amnesia to have a certainty of anything, but tomorrow she would go to Lackington, Allen & Co. and look up the files under the medical section of the library. Knowledge would aid her.

Perhaps she could help him redefine his memory. But should she? Would her presence at his side, even in that capacity, put her own self into danger?

She needed to wait, she thought. She needed to see just how the next few days turned out in order to make an informed decision about her and Lucy's future.

He did not wear his crested ring any more. He did not smile as he used to. She wondered if he was financially strapped with his hair and his clothes and his scuffed old boots. There had been talk of his inheritances passing on to his uncle given the number of years of his being away. Perhaps being presumed dead even negated legal rights to property?

Many *had* thought him dead, after all. She had heard it in the drawing rooms of society and in the quieter salons of the *ton*. The dashing and dissolute young Viscount Bromley's disappearance was mourned by myriad feminine hearts and the gold coins he had lost in the seedier halls of London's gambling scene had only added to his allure. He was now touted as a legend whose deeds had only been enhanced by the mystery surrounding him.

Eleanor could not even imagine him in society looking like he did now. No one would recognise him. People would pity him. The scar at his cheek, the injured hand and the uncertainty. He would be crucified within the hallowed snobbery of the *ton*!

How could she protect him?

By staying in London and being there to

pick up the pieces, perhaps? By sending Lucy home to Millbrook House with her nanny and maids tomorrow until she was certain which way the dice tumbled?

Oh, God, now she was thinking at the opposite spectrum of what she had started to decide. Stay away from Nicholas entirely or try to protect him? Which was it to be? Which *should* it be?

Underneath her thoughts a small flame flared, then took and filled her whole body with gladness. These arguments were all academic because now he was alive to her again. Nicholas Bartlett, Viscount Bromley, was not dead. He was here and breathing, the past covering him like a dull shroud, but nevertheless still quick.

Everything was possible whilst life bloomed and her brother and his friends would not desert him. She knew that from what Jacob had said. Placing her hands together she prayed.

'Give thanks in all circumstances; for this is God's will for you...' Thessalonians again. She murmured the scripture into the silence with an emotion that she found both comforting and worrying.

Tonight she would dream of him just as she had done a thousand times since he had disappeared, his arms around her body and his warm lips covering her own.

But this time it would be different for he was no longer just a ghost.

Frederick's carriage collected him the next morning well before the luncheon and when he arrived at the home of the Challengers in St James's Square, Nick understood just how happy his friend was these days.

Georgiana, Fred's wife, was gracious and welcoming even with the house in an uproar as it made itself ready for the evening's entertainment.

'It is a pleasure to meet you, Lord Bromley.' A real smile touched her blue eyes and although she did not look at his scar, she did not look away from it either. 'I have heard much about you for Frederick has spoken of you so very often.'

'I hope he concentrated on my good qualities rather than the bad ones.' He tried to keep his tone light.

'The wildness of youth is never easy, I fear, and often misrepresented, but rest assured my husband has missed you.'

In such wisdom Nick detected that Georgiana's life might have had its own complexities and he wondered about her story.

Half an hour later when he and Fred were alone in the library and a drink had been poured, Nick put his head back against the leather rest of a large wing chair and took in breath.

'Your wife has the knack of making this all look easy,' he said finally. 'A house of things being both interesting and alive, but without the chaos of your upbringing? Where did you meet her?'

'I first saw her at Vitium et Virtus late one night when she was auctioning off her virginity to the highest bidder, wearing nothing more than a silk concoction that was barely decent.'

Nick laughed at that and liked the sound of it. 'And I gather that the winner of such an unusual prize was yourself?'

'Fortunately.'

They both took a drink and listened to the low rumbling noise of the busy house.

'Georgie was promised in marriage to Sir Nash Bowles and doing her level best to get out of it. It was the only plan she could think of. Unwise but spectacularly successful.' Frederick's laugh was deep.

'Bowles was there? At the club?'

'He was.' Fred had sobered now at mention of that name, the good humour of a second ago fading markedly.

'One of the last things I remember is warning him to never darken its door again, but he obviously returned.'

'My wife sees him as perverted and cruel.'

'And I would agree with her.'

'Well, the one thing I do thank him for is his threats to unmask her completely. It was only because she thought she might be shunned as a pariah when the *ton* got wind of her improper plan that she agreed to marry me.'

'A wise choice.' Nick lifted his glass and finished the brandy before placing it down on the table beside him and refusing Frederick's offer of another. 'The world you all live in has changed a lot since I have been gone.'

'And you have changed in appearance since last night. Jacob's barber is a magician, by the way.'

'The bath helped, too. The Westmoor physician also came this morning to see to my hand. He says he expects it to heal completely if I am careful.'

'Knife wounds can be difficult things.'

'The blade hit the bone at the back of the wrist, but at least it did not break.'

'Which explains the sling. If you don't want to be thrown into society so quickly by coming tonight, Nick, I will understand. After the army it was hard for me to fit straight back in.'

'Because you felt different? Out of place?'

'Yes, and because I had seen things that no one else could even imagine.'

Frederick was quiet then and Nicholas was glad of it.

'I had thought to go to ground, but if I don't come tonight it will only get harder. Better to get it over and done with. I saw Lady Eleanor yesterday, too, by the way.' He tried to keep interest out of his words though he was not certain he had succeeded as Frederick looked up. 'What is her story?'

'Jake is very tight lipped about his sister, but from what I can gather the man she married was from a well-thought-of family in Edinburgh. The Robertsons.'

'Was it the family of the Robertson boy we knew at school, then?'

'No, by all accounts he was not related to them. Douglas Robertson, Eleanor's husband, was killed falling off a horse, apparently in some hunting accident, and when Eleanor found out she was pregnant she came home to Millbrook to have her baby daughter, Lucy. And to grieve.'

Lucy. Nick stored the name inside him and thought how hard a path that must have been for a sheltered duke's daughter with all the promise in the world.

A bit like him, perhaps, although his promise had been dimming even before his absence from England. His uncle had encouraged him into the profligate and debauched underworld of the *ton* and he had gone in to welcome the inherent risks with his eyes wide open.

'Do you ever think, Fred, that maybe we were fools back then, playing so hard and fast?'

'I think you and Oliver were the ones who were the worst of us although you held the biggest share in Vitium et Virtus and gambled away the most money.'

'It was fun until it wasn't,' he returned and stood to look out of the window. 'I will go up to Bromworth House tomorrow and see my uncle.'

'Take my carriage.'

'Oliver offered me the use of his yesterday.'

'Will you live there this time, do you think? Put down roots and stay?'

Nicholas shrugged his shoulders because he truly did not know.

'My advice would be to find a wife like mine, Nick. A woman who can be the better half of you, for without Georgiana at my side I'd still be lost.'

As I am, Nicholas thought, and felt the shiver of ghosts walk down his spine.

Frederick leant forward, swirling the brandy around in his glass. 'We can move the club on into other hands, younger ones. It's probably past time.'

'Do you have anyone in mind?'

'Half the upcoming bucks of the *ton* would jump to it in a second, but it has to be the right people. A group of friends like us maybe, people who could work together.' He smiled, his brown eyes soft. 'For so long we all feared you were dead, Nick. For so long we talked of you with sorrow and regret even as we relived your wildest exploits. It is good to have you back again and in one piece.'

'Well, perhaps not quite one piece, Frederick.' That truth settled between them.

'The bits will come back to you, but give it time and don't force it. One day you will rise in the morning and realise life is easier and that the demons that once threatened to engulf you are more distant.'

'Less insistent?'

'Then you will also understand that life carries on, different from before maybe but still valuable, and that there are people in the world who never stopped loving you. Myself included.'

Frederick waited until he nodded before carrying on.

'But enough of this maudlin emotion and confession, for I think we now need to get down to this afternoon's business and find you some more appropriate clothes to wear.'

Thus the mundane allowed an end to the extraordinary truths of the conversation.

Nicholas could not remember ever taking this long to dress, but the Challenger valet was both insistent and persuasive and, although he had no clothes of his own to speak of, the man soon conjured up an array of cast-offs that fitted him well.

'Just a slight tuck here, my lord.' His grip was firm on the side seam of the jacket. 'You don't quite have the girth of Major Challenger. The trousers have been lengthened, but a good steam has taken care of any tell-tale signs of alteration. They give a fine impression of being your own clothes, Lord Bromley. Tailored to perfection if I might say so myself.'

'Thank you.' He gave this quietly. It had been years since he had had a servant fuss over him in such a way and it made him feel strangely odd. He had never given those who worked for the Bromley estate much thought before, but now he did. He hoped his uncle had treated them well and that there might be a few familiar faces at the Manor when he went up there on the morrow.

The luxury of London unsettled him and he fought for a touchstone. He wondered if Eleanor Huntingdon might come to Frederick's soirée with her brother. He would like to see her dressed in finery with her hair arranged to show off the colour of it. He would like to dance with her. He would like to have her near.

Frederick came into the room he had been assigned just as the valet had finished the last stitch and broken off the thread, smoothing down the fabric.

'A fine job, Masters. The Viscount looks as though he should fit in nicely.'

When the man collected all the assorted

spools and left, Fred poured them each some wine in ornate cut-crystal glasses.

'For fortification,' he said and raised the tipple. 'Most of those present tonight are friends and acquaintances, but there are always the certain few outsiders who might want to rock the boat.'

'Are you warning me, Fred?'

'You've been away a long time and stories have formed around your disappearance that have no bearing on the truth.'

'For that I am glad.'

'But a word of advice. If you do not wish to be the continued censure of the gossipmongers perhaps you could think of a reason for your injuries that may be more palatable. An army wound? The sanctity of government violence goes a long way in suppressing criticism, I have always found. The Seminole Wars, perhaps? The time frame would fit.'

'You have thought about this already?'

When Frederick began to laugh he did, too.

'The legends that abound about you as the reckless and dissolute Viscount Bromley are also a protection. No one will know quite who you are.'

'Including me.' He said the words quietly and finished his drink.

Frederick's frown was deep. 'You can't do this alone any more, Nick. You have to let us all help you.'

'You are already doing that and I will be fine.'

Chapter Four

Eleanor had dressed as carefully as she ever had, her maids watching her with puzzlement on both their faces. Usually she barely cared. Normally if she went out it was only with much chagrin that she suffered even an hour of the business of 'getting ready'.

Today she had spent most of the afternoon changing her mind from this dress to that one, from a formal hair style to a far less structured one. Even her shoes had been swapped from one pair to the next.

And now with only a few moments before she needed to go downstairs and join her brother and sister-in-law she was still unsure. Was the gold of her gown a little gaudy? Did her hair, set into up-pulled ringlets, look contrived? Was the diamond choker at her throat too much of a statement for a woman of her age?

She looked away from her reflection and breathed in deeply. No more. No other changes. She was exhausted by her uncertainty.

Jacob smiled as he saw her descending the staircase.

'I have not seen you look quite as beautiful for a very long time, Ellie.'

Rose beside him looked as pleased as her brother did. 'It is going to be so lovely to have you with us at Frederick and Georgiana's, Eleanor. I wish you were with us more often in London.' Her sister-in-law was in blue tonight and her fairness made her look like an angel. Every time Eleanor saw Rose she could understand exactly what her brother had seen in her as a choice of wife. She was kind and quiet, a woman who did not push herself forward, but waited for others to come to her.

With a laugh Eleanor took the offered hand and felt immeasurably more confident, an emotion she would need if she were to be any help to Nicholas Bartlett.

'Nick has gone on already,' Jacob said. 'Frederick had a set of clothes that he needed to see if he fitted and he wanted Nicholas to meet Georgiana before this evening's function.'

'I am sure the Viscount will look well in anything he chooses. From all the accounts

I have heard from my maid this morning as I was dressing he is a most handsome man.'

Rose's statement was firm and Eleanor glanced at her. She herself had not seen Nicholas Bartlett in the house all day as he had left in the mid-morning for the Challengers. She hoped he had found a barber at least to shave off his beard.

Her nerves started to make her worried again. If people were rude or worse to him she could not quite think what she would do. Her brother would hardly tolerate such behaviour, of course, but still there was a difference between being accepted for who you were and being gossiped about behind raised fans and turned heads.

'I hope Lord Bromley will enjoy himself,' she finally said and left it at that.

It was only a short ride from Chelsea to St James's Square and the rain and wind had held off enough to allow them a quiet passage into the house. After the death of her brother and father the family had been largely in mourning so it felt good to be able to go out again. The Challenger soirée would have a lot of people who were known to them attending, but it was not as formal as some of the grander balls.

Frederick and Georgiana Challenger were there to greet them after their cloaks, hats and gloves were seen to. Eleanor was, as always, struck anew at just how fine they looked together as they welcomed the newcomers.

'Oliver was unable to make it tonight, Jake, because Cecilia is not very well. Nick is inside, but the doctor wanted his hand up in a sling so we had to rearrange his shirt and jacket somewhat.'

Another problem, Eleanor thought. A further way to draw attention to his differences. She suddenly wished she had stayed home.

The large downstairs salon of the Challenger town house was completely decked out in yellow, the colour lightening the space and making it seem even bigger. Numerous people milled around the room in groups and at one end an orchestra was tuning up with a Christmas song, 'Hark the Herald Angels Sing'. Eleanor had always liked the melody.

'I thought Frederick said this was to be a small gathering,' Rose remarked. 'It seems half the *ton* is here tonight.'

Eleanor looked around trying to find the figure of Nicholas Bartlett. At six foot two his height should have had him standing a good head above many of the others, but she could not see him.

Perhaps he had cried off and left?

'There is Nicholas. Over by the pillars.' Her brother's voice penetrated her reveries as he pushed through the crowd and once the crush thinned a little she saw the Viscount surrounded by women and men all hanging on to his every word.

Her first true sight of him took her breath away. He looked completely different from yesterday. Menacing, dangerously beautiful, the boy she had known fashioned into the man before her, the harder lines of his face without the full beard suiting him in a way she had not comprehended before.

He was all in black, save for the snowy cravat at his neck, folded simply. His hair was pulled into a severe queue and she could see the sheen of dark brown picked out under the chandeliers above them.

His left hand was fastened into a sling of linen, the small vulnerability suiting him in a way she had not thought would be possible—a warrior who had been into battle and returned triumphant. She could see in his velvet eyes an apartness that left him unmatched. Every man near him looked soft, tame and pliable. Untouched by danger and hardship.

Their party had to squeeze into the space about him and Eleanor noticed the frowns of those women who had hoped for a closer acquaintance as they were ousted back.

'You have cleaned up well, Nick. I hardly recognise you in the man we saw yesterday.' Jacob sounded relieved. 'I would like to introduce you to Rose, my wife. You did not meet her this morning before you left.'

Rose looked tiny compared to the Viscount, his darkness contrasting, too, against her light hair and eyes. Eleanor watched as Nicholas Bartlett brought up her sister-in-law's hand and kissed the back of it, his gallantry reminiscent of the younger man who had left them all those years before. A slide of anger turned inside Eleanor as he acknowledged her with a mere tip of his head and yet he made a space at his side and she came to stand there, making very sure that she did not touch him.

'I hope you slept well last night, Lady Eleanor.' He said this to her as Rose and Jacob were busy in conversation with an older lord they knew well. An allusion to their late-night meeting, she supposed. Unexpectedly she coloured and hated herself for doing so.

'I did, thank you.' In truth, she had gained about three hours' sleep and it probably showed in the darkness under her eyes. He, on the other hand, looked as if he had slept like a baby.

'Frederick said there would be dancing later in the evening. Might I petition you to save one for me?'

'I am rather out of practice, my lord.' She could not keep the surprise from her tone.

'And you think I wouldn't be?'

'I do not know. I have no idea of what sort of life you lived in the Americas.'

At that he sobered.

As the crowd about them jostled slightly Mr Alfred Dromorne and his daughter broke in on their conversation.

'Bromley. It has been a long time. May I introduce my daughter to you. She is recently out in society. Susan, this is Viscount Bromley.'

Nicholas Bartlett inclined his head at the beautiful girl standing next to her father, though his eyes were far less readable than they had been a second ago. It was as if a shutter had been placed over any true expression and the fingers she could see that were visible in the sling had curled in tension.

The vibrant red head smiled in the way only the very young and very beautiful know how to. All coquetry and cunning. Eleanor felt instantly older and a lot more dowdy than she had even a second before.

'I am pleased to meet you, Miss Dromorne.'

'And I you, my lord.' She brought her fan up and twirled it a few times, the art of flirtation both complex and simple in its execution.

'You will be going home to Bromworth Manor, no doubt, now that you are back. You might notice some changes to the place.'

Her father had taken up the conversation and his statement produced a flicker of genuine interest in Lord Bromley's visage. Eleanor saw the eagerness even as he sought to hide it.

'In what ways do you mean?

'Your uncle has the run of the estate these days and he has made certain to stamp his authority on to the place. Last time I was there I rather thought that those still serving him were not entirely happy.'

'Large estates have their problems,' Nicholas replied, giving the distinct impression that he did not wish to discuss such personal matters with a stranger. Eleanor noticed, too, that the pulse at his throat had quickened markedly.

'You promised Lord Craybourne that you would be back to talk with him and I see he is free now, Lord Bromley. Perhaps this would be a good time.'

'It would.' With a slight bow to the Dromornes he allowed Eleanor to lead the way across the floor, though once they were out of sight she felt his hand on her arm stopping her.

She turned and saw right into his tortured soul, the lack of reserve astonishing.

'Are you ill, my lord?'

He looked away and swallowed hard. She had the distinct impression that should she leave him here in the middle of the crowded floor he might very well simply fall over.

Knowing the Challengers' town house as well as she did, she gestured to a room off to one side, glad when he followed her and the door shut behind them.

'I think you should sit down, Lord Bromley.'

He did that, immediately, and closed his eyes.

'I have been alone for a very long time. It takes some getting used to, this crush of people.'

'It was not like this in the Americas?'

'I kept away from others there.'

His words to her brother in the library last night came back. *'It is dangerous, Jake. If anything were to happen to you and your family...'*

He was trapped in his life as surely as she was.

'You think you might cause those around you harm? Even here in England?'

At that he opened his eyes and leant back. 'I know so.'

'Is it your uncle? Is it his doing?'

'He has the motivation, but...'

'You think it is another?'

For the first time in a long while Nicholas felt his intuition kick in fervently. Eleanor Huntingdon made him alive again in a way no one else did. He barely knew her, but there was something between them that felt right and strong.

'I have many other enemies. Some I probably don't even remember.'

'That sounds dangerous. To not have recall of people who might hurt you, I mean. Is Dromorne one of those enemies?'

'Perhaps. He is a friend of my uncle, Mr Aaron Bartlett, who now sets himself up in

Bromworth Manor with the intention of taking both my title and inheritance.'

'Why would he introduce his daughter to you, then? He looked as if he wished for you to take the acquaintance with his offspring a lot further.'

'To hedge his bets, perhaps. A pound on my uncle and another on me. The Bromley assets are substantial.'

'A gambling man? No true morality in him?'

'I remember that I owe Dromorne money. No doubt he will be calling upon it as soon as he can.'

There was now a dark cloud of worry in Eleanor's eyes as he told her this.

'Could I give you some advice?' He fashioned the words with care and was pleased when she nodded.

'You should probably stay well away from me, Lady Eleanor. The man I used to be was not much, but this one is even more...' Struggling for a word he gave up and left the implication hanging.

'Perilous?' Her smile surprised him as did the quick flare of anger. 'That may very well be true, but you offered me a dance a few moments ago and I shall hold you to your promise. The quadrille is my favourite, Lord Bromley.'

He felt better even looking at her, the gold of her gown picking up the sky blue of her eyes. 'I shall find you then when I hear the tune struck. And thank you.' He gazed around the room.

'My pleasure, but I think I must go now or the others will miss me.'

She had left before he could give her his response and the night dulled with her absence, but he needed the solitude, too, to recoup and recover. He hoped that there were not others here who would pounce on his memory. The medicines Jacob's physician had given him for his arm were making him feel sick. Sick in body and in mind. This evening was a lot more tiring than he had thought it would be and he was only glad that Eleanor Huntingdon had recognised the desperation in him and found him sanctuary.

He tried in earnest to bring to mind the steps of the quadrille she had mentioned, hoping that he might manage it without tipping both of them over.

The face of his uncle also hovered above him, a man whom he had never liked. Looking back, Nick knew he should have heaved him out of his life when his majority was reached, but he had been too self-destructive to even bother, his days revolving around the fast London set, Vitium et Virtus and gambling.

A mistake, he thought now, looking back. He would see his man of business and his lawyer as soon as he could to find out where he stood with his inheritance. But a day or two away in the quiet English countryside might be just what he needed and the sooner he got rid of his father's scheming younger brother from influencing any part of his future, the better.

The hours seemed to have flown by at this soirée of Frederick's. Nicholas Bartlett had not come near her again, but she had watched him across the other side of the room, ensconced in a group of admirers both female and male.

He looked much recovered, she thought, and the fact that her brother and Frederick Challenger were there beside him probably had something to do with that.

Rose, next to her, saw where she was looking. 'There is something about Lord Bromley that makes him fascinating, do you not

think? He looks both vulnerable and dangerous, a man whose history sits upon him with
weight.'

'Did Jacob tell you of his time in the Americas?'

'A little. He said the Viscount was always
moving to the next place of work and that he
had a hard life there. I think people here are
watching to find the careless dissolute lord
they used to know, for the young girls certainly have their eyes on him. But he does
not seem to be rising to any expectation and
that is what is causing a quandary. Who is he
now seems to be the general question. Did
you know him well before he left, Eleanor?
Can you see similarities with who he is now?'

Eleanor ignored the first question and answered the second. 'I think he was a lot less
dangerous and more easily swayed perhaps.'

Nicholas Bartlett tipped his head as she
said this and looked straight at her, across
the distance of the room, across the music and
the movement and the chatter and it was as
if the tableau of everything faded. Only him.
Only her. Only the memory of what had been.
Her memory, but not his. She looked away
and fidgeted with her reticule, hating the way
her fingers shook as she reached for her fan.

'Do you ever imagine yourself marrying again, Ellie?' Rose's voice was soft.

'Why do you ask?'

'Because you are a beautiful woman with much to offer a man.'

'No.' The word burst from her very being, the truth of such emotion worrying. Because she did not. If she could not have Nicholas Bartlett to love her again as he had done before then she did not want anyone. Ever.

'Secrets can be lonely things, Eleanor. If you wish to talk…'

Rose left it there as they both looked across to watch the orchestra tune up for their next round of songs and then the Viscount was right next to her, holding out his hand.

'You promised me a dance, Lady Eleanor, and I have come to claim it.'

'I think this one is a waltz, sir,' she clarified, hearing the tell-tale three-beat music.

'Good,' he returned, 'for I am sure I can remember those steps.'

'And your injured hand?' When she looked she saw he had taken off the sling in readiness, only the bandage left, a snowy white against the dark edge of the cuff of his jacket.

'The doctor assured me that if needs be

I could remove the sling without too much harm.'

He had not danced at all that evening and she could see the interest in those around them as he made his way to the floor with her in tow. Her brother was watching, as was Rose and myriad other faces from further afield.

'One turn about the floor shall not drag you into the mire of who I am, I think. It should be safe.'

His fingers were at her side now, the other injured hand coming carefully on to hers. She could feel his breath in her hair as he counted in the steps and see up close the damage done to his face.

He did not try to hide it from her and she liked that, but the scar was substantial and re-cent, the reddened edges of it only just knitted.

'The wife of the owner of the tavern I worked at sewed it up for me.' He said this when he saw her observing him. 'She was an accomplished seamstress so I was lucky.'

'Lucky…' she echoed his word.

'Not to die from it. Lucky to have escaped a second blow and still live.'

'What happened to the man who did this to you?'

When he glanced at her and she saw the

darkness in his eyes she knew exactly what had happened to his assailant.

A further difference. Another danger.

'Scars can be hidden, too, Lord Bromley.'

The upturn of his mouth told her he had heard her whisper even when he did not answer.

'And rest assured that in a room like this there will be people who have been hurt just as surely as you.'

'But they have not the luck to dance with the most beautiful woman in the house.'

'I think your eyesight must have suffered with your injury.'

'Gold suits you.'

She was quiet.

'So does silence.'

At that she laughed, because thus far since meeting him again she had voiced her opinion without reserve. He made her talk again. He made her take risks.

He was quickly catching on to the rhythm of the dance and manoeuvred her easily about the room despite the number of others on the floor. She could feel hardness in his body where before there had been softness. He smelt of lemon soap and cleanliness, the lack of any other perfume refreshing.

At five foot six she was quite tall for a woman. With him she felt almost tiny, her head fitting easily into the space beneath his chin. Breathing him in, she allowed him to lead her, closing her eyes for a second just to feel what she once had at the Bromley town house the night before his disappearance. The night Lucy was conceived.

She had sent Lucy away today, back to Millbrook, just so that as a mother she might understand the road she must now travel.

Towards him or away? The quick squeeze of his fingers against hers brought her eyes up to his own, an emotion there she could not interpret.

'A lack of memory is a hard taskmaster,' he whispered, 'because sometimes I imagine...' He stopped.

'What? What do you imagine?'

'That I have danced with you before.'

She looked away and hated the lump that had formed in the back of her throat.

The night lights of the city had glowed through the large sashed windows of his town house as he had taken her into his arms and danced her to his bed.

Please remember, she thought. Please remember and love me. Then Mr Dromorne's face at the side of the floor came into view, watching with eyes that held no warmth whatsoever and as the music ran down into the final notes Nicholas escorted her back to her brother.

She did not see him again that evening, but knew he had gone into the card room because the whispers of his luck there began to float into the salon.

An hour later when Rose pleaded tiredness, Eleanor was more than grateful to accompany her home.

Nicholas sat with a whisky in his room and listened to the clock strike the hour of five. The fire in the grate was still ablaze for he had fed it for all the small hours of the early morning with the coal piled near the hearth in a shining copper holder.

Eleanor Huntingdon was asleep somewhere in the house and close. He wished they could talk again. He wished he could see her smile and hear her clever honest words.

He had paid off Dromorne with a good percentage of his takings so that was one creditor he no longer had to worry about. His skill at cards had risen directly with the practice he'd had in the Americas.

The basic strategy of the games had become like second nature to him, the running number of points holding little difficulty. He could count down a single deck to zero within ten seconds in order to know exactly where his edge lay.

A dubious talent and one that told others much about the life he had lived in the interim. He had seen Jacob and Frederick watching him with questions in their eyes. He was only glad that Jacob's sister had retired early because this acquired skill was not attractive.

He would need to leave for Bromworth Manor soon. That thought had him swallowing more of his whisky and standing to look out of the window.

The orderliness of London was what had struck him first on his return. The neat lines of houses and the straight roads. The lights added to the illusion that the city went on for ever, stretching from east to west in a long and unbroken tableau. Virginia and Georgia and the Carolinas had been wild and lonely places. Sometimes he had walked between settlements for a week or more and seen no one.

Tonight he had panicked badly in that room of Frederick's with almost a hundred people in it and Eleanor had noticed and helped him. If she had not been there he wondered what might have happened. If she had not led him to that secluded room, he had no faith in thinking he would have coped.

He did not trust himself any more to act accordingly, to function here, to blend in with the *ton* whilst he tried to understand just who it was here who meant him harm.

If it was his uncle then it would be easy to negate any danger, but Eleanor's question had set his mind running in other directions.

'You think it is another?'

His father's brother might have the motivation to see him dead in England, but he doubted the man had the drive or the contacts to send someone after him to the Americas. If it was not him, then it would need to be an enemy with a good deal of money to spare and a large axe to grind. He could think of any number of past acquaintances who might have fitted that bill given his debauched behaviour as a young viscount of means.

His sins were returning to roost. If he could only remember his missing week, he thought, he might know the perpetrator, but not one drip of recall had come through the solid curtain of mist.

He needed to sleep to be focused on his

journey later that day and yet he did not seek his bed. Rather he stood and watched the moon and the sky and the cold gleam of freshly falling snow on the roadway in front of the Westmoor town house, his isolation making him shiver.

Chapter Five

❧❧❧

Bromworth Manor was exactly as he remembered, the dark trees that ran along the drive towards it as forbidding as they always had been with their twisted limbs and branches.

The family seat stood proud before a wooded hill overlooking an ornamental lake. Built for defence in the early fourteenth century, the remains of a moat and drawbridge could still be seen to one side, the stonework on this part of the building cruder and darker than its paler, more modern counterpart.

After the onset of the Palladian style a different profile had arisen around the fortress that was more beautiful and substantial. With its pale stone, large rounded windows and double-storeyed wings, Bromworth held the semblance of grandeur, history and wealth.

His direct ancestors had lived here for hundreds of years. It was an estate that spoke of family and celebrations as well as defeats and tragedy. He remembered some of the portraits that lined the walls in the lower hall with a smile. Lovers, soldiers, keepers of the law were displayed there, each Viscount and his family afforded a position in the marching changes of history.

His own visage had not been recorded. He had been very young when his parents had died and later, when a portrait might have been commissioned, he'd wanted little to do with the place at all.

He remembered the local chaplain coming with one of the women from the church in the nearest village, their faces strained in concern as their words tumbled out, banishing his parents to another realm. A quick and final malady that had come on late one night while they were from home and left them both dead by the next. No hope to it. He was an orphan now with a guardian in the form of an uncle he barely knew.

At eight he had had a hard time of imagining the concept of 'for ever lost' though it had soon started to impress itself on all the various strands of his life and he had rebelled against his new punitive reality with every fibre of his being.

The first loss was the hardest, but there had been so many more since then. He was wearing Jacob's boots and Frederick's clothes and the winnings left over from yesterday's card game was the only money in his pocket. Oliver had lent him a carriage and driver for the journey to Essex.

He'd become a jigsaw of other people's lives, the hard, distant core of him hidden from everyone. A man alone and struggling with it.

The front portal creaked open before he had knocked and old Ramsey the butler stood there, his face showing a number of emotions before settling into a smile.

'Lord Bromley.' The man's mouth worked as he tried to say other things, but could not. In the end the servant stepped forward and grabbed his hand, the tight warmth in the shake reassuring. 'I cannot believe it is you, my lord. After all this time you are finally come home.'

'Is Mr Bartlett in, Ramsey?'

'He calls himself Lord Bromley now, my lord.' That was given with a worried glance. 'He believes you dead.'

'Where is he?'

'In bed, I should imagine. He rarely rises before the noon hour and it is not yet that.'

'Can you take me to him?'

'With pleasure, my lord.'

The man waved away a younger servant who stood behind him, stuck out his chest and walked to the large and winding staircase. 'He has your old suite of rooms, Lord Bromley.'

As they went Nicholas saw many of the paintings that lined the stairway had been changed. Dark, sombre strangers now peered down at him. After he tossed his uncle out of Bromworth Manor these would be the next things to go.

The bedchamber was dull and muted, the curtains not yet drawn. Without glancing at the bed, Nick crossed to the windows and threw the shades back. The light fell on the man resting against his pillows, older now, but still as mean spirited and bad tempered as he always had been, his face suffused by a number of changing emotions.

'You. But you are dead.'

'Not quite, Uncle, though I imagine you to have had some say in the fact that I nearly was.'

'Some say? Says who?' Aaron Bartlett threw

his head back and frowned as he pushed back the covers. Both cheeks were aflame with rosacea and his jowls had markedly thickened. He looked nothing at all like his brother.

'Those who hit me in the back alley of Vitium et Virtus mentioned your name. They said it was you who had sent them.' It was a lie, of course, as Nick had no memory of any of it, but his friends had told him the story of the pool of blood and the retrieval of his signet ring so he took the gamble. 'You wanted the Bromley inheritances enough to kill for them.'

The man opposite him had his feet to the floor now and sat. The shake in his hands could be seen easily even at this distance across the room. In his white nightgown he looked both a pathetic figure and a powerless one. For the first time he also looked frightened.

'The men I sent to the alley were paid to merely scare you off. You cannot prove I meant to kill you. No court in the land would try me on that. You were out of control with your gambling and I was trying to stop you from ruining everything.'

'After encouraging me in it for all the years before?'

'The Bromley fortune, whilst rich, was not limitless and you rarely won after the first few flushes.'

'So you sent assassins after me to the Americas in order to keep what was left?'

'I dispatched no one across the ocean. Why should I have done so? You were already gone. Drowned in the Thames.'

Such a confession sat congealing in the thick air of the chamber, a truth that held nothing in it save betrayal.

'Get your things and leave. You have my permission to use the Bromley carriage to take what you can carry away from here, but after this there will be nothing.'

Nick was furious and shocked, the numbness of his uncle's treachery creeping into coldness.

'Nothing? Nothing?' Bartlett stood now and bellowed the two words.

'Less than nothing if you argue.' His reply was quiet. 'You have half an hour. After that I will have my servants throw you out.'

'You cannot do that, for God's sake. Your father wished for me to be a figure in your life…'

'A cantankerous, avaricious greedy bastard is not what I imagine he had in mind and I owe you less than nothing. You are dead to me. A man who could have chosen a better path, but didn't.' He pointedly looked at his timepiece. 'Twenty-nine minutes now.'

At that Nick turned, ignoring the run of insults that followed him to the door as he shut it behind him and took in a breath. It was over. Aaron Bartlett was out of his life.

Exactly half an hour later his uncle stood before him, hastily dressed and furious.

'This is not the end of this, mark my words. There will be legalities to deal with and the fact that you were all but dead for so many years—'

Nicholas had had enough of his threats and, grabbing him by his shirt front, he hauled his uncle off his feet.

'If you ever darken my door again, I won't be as kind as I have been this time, do you understand? My advice would be to leave England before any creditors know you have gone, for this way you have a chance of leaving the country alive. If you stay, I will find you and deal with you as you dealt with me.'

'You were out of control and reckless…'

'Enough.'

This time Bartlett blanched white and was

silent and Nick, releasing his hold, allowed the butler to show Bartlett out. A few moments later Nick heard the movement of the carriage and the call of the driver.

Gone.

He thought back to all the moments he had hated his uncle and felt no remorse at all. His guardian was a heart-dead greedy sycophant, but worse than that he was immoral. He still held the thin scars on his arms where he'd been whipped time after time as a child when he had refused direction.

The grave of the family dog his guardian had had shot was marked in the woods by all the shale and stones that Nicholas himself had buried him under, each one drenched in tears.

His uncle had made him into a young man of wildness and anger, the responsibilities of love and family lost under greed.

'Could I pour you a drink, Lord Bromley? There are some fine reds from your father's collection that we managed to hide.'

Ramsey looked both worried and relieved. 'We have been waiting for your return, you see, my lord, for the reappearance of a master who was not…so immoral, I mean. Mrs Ramsey has ham and fresh bread in the kitchens should you wish for it and the chutney this year was particularly tasty.'

'Thank you.' When Nick looked at him closely there were tears in the old butler's eyes. 'I would like that.'

Ten minutes later he was sitting in front of a roaring fire in the large kitchen, the fare of the county on the table before him and an uncorked bottle of his father's burgundy.

A row of servants stood behind him, some known and some new. All looked tense and uncertain.

'Find another few more glasses, Ramsey, and we will all partake in a toast.'

He had never once in his years at Bromworth Manor spoken so familiarly to the staff and he had never before been in this room, the very heart of the place.

He was once again lord of Bromworth Manor and lord of these lands, but there had been a shift inside him. He felt more comfortable with these people than he did with the gossiping aristocrats of the *ton*. He felt at home here, a belonging, a place to put down roots and stay.

The very feeling calmed him and made him lighter. For the first time ever he felt he was following in the footsteps of his beloved father.

The land held an ancient history, carried down by the centuries, of planting and nurturing. Perhaps it was the same with people? The rain, the soil, the forests, the hills. They were imprinted within him, known and familiar, a part of his understanding in the translation of life.

In the Americas it had all been so foreign. Different seas and rivers and plants. Foreign languages and foods that he had no understanding of or liking for.

The codes for being a Bromley had been ripped out of him, forgotten, lost in violence and circumstance. Here, the pattern reformed and carried on, the smells of the place, the sounds, the shadows and the light.

A comradeship. A rightness.

He picked up the cheese knife and looked at the crested end of it. *Servire Populo*. For the first time ever he understood exactly what it meant.

Much later he walked down to the small graveyard behind the ruined chapel, the stones of commemoration ill kept and unweeded.

He found his parents' graves side by side

in one corner, the late winter sun still upon them, and he was glad for it.

His fingers traced the words that he knew by heart. Their names. The dates of their births and deaths. The epitaph was short. Chosen by his uncle, he guessed, and conveying little.

Until we meet again.

The words made him smile as he imagined his father with his hands around the throat of his brother in an eternal celestial retribution when he arrived at the heavenly gates for judgement.

Placing the wildflowers he had gathered on his mother's stone, he bowed his head.

Today he felt closer to them than he had felt in years.

'I will become a better man.' The words were out before he knew them said, slipping into the breeze, though when his good hand dug into his pocket to try to banish the cold he felt the hard outline of a set of dice. His injured hand ached with the effort of lifting Bartlett, but it was worth it.

People arrived at the place they were meant to be even if they came with a past. It was how life worked. But the past did not have to define one just as the present did not. The future was his, here in Essex, in the ancient seat of the Bromleys. It was his to nurture, grow and tend to.

Hope filled him. For Bromworth, for a new direction, for his friends and their support.

For Eleanor Huntingdon.

That name had him tensing. They barely knew one another, but she was there none the less in his mind, her smile, the way she spoke, the vivid blue of her eyes and the dark of her hair.

He would like to show her this estate. He would like to walk with her and tell her all that had happened to him, as a child, as a youth, as a man, so that she might know of the darkness inside him.

Of all the people in the world he thought she would be the one to understand.

Eleanor sat in the library at the Westmoor town house, stitching a complex tapestry of colourful nasturtiums, although her heart was not in it.

At every noise outside she stopped to listen, every sound of horses and carriage, every call of a night bird or the far-off ringing of bells.

Her brother and Rose had gone to a play

at the Royal Coburg Theatre, but she knew Nicholas Bartlett was expected back from Essex tonight. She hoped it might be when the others were absent for she wanted to speak with him privately and make him an offer.

An offer. Even the words sounded impossibly difficult.

Placing down her stitching, she pulled back the fabric of her bodice and lifted up the gold chain that she always wore around her neck. The small ring brought a smile to her lips as her fingers closed about it.

Blue zircon had a charm more captivating than the sophisticated diamonds which it sometimes imitated.

They had found it in a jewellery shop in Piccadilly on the day they had visited Lackington, Allen & Co. and Nicholas had purchased the trinket because the colour matched her eyes exactly.

'Like blue starlight,' he had said and she'd laughed, because of the fancy and daydream.

She had worn it then on the third finger of her right hand, a troth, a promise, a way to the future that she could see so very easily before her.

And even when he had disappeared she could not bear to have it away from her skin and so she had fastened it to a fragile chain her father had made her a gift of on her fifteenth birthday and she had worn it there every day since.

She looked at the clock. Half past nine. Perhaps the Viscount was not returning from Bromworth Manor tonight after all. Perhaps things had gone awry with the uncle that her brother had said Nicholas had gone to expel from the family estate. Perhaps there had been a fight or an accident on the road like her father and Ralph had had. She shook that thought away.

Jacob had told her this morning that Nicholas was almost certain his guardian had been the one to waylay him in the alley. After today there would be no more looking over one's shoulder and expecting trouble, for if he knew the perpetrator of all his problems he could deal with the man summarily. She breathed out with decided relief and was pleased for the decisions she had made last night to help Nicholas Bartlett with his lost week.

Noises came through the quiet and then there was the sound of horses and bustle, a called-out goodbye and footsteps leading up the steps. After that the front door closed behind the newcomer and his voice reached her with its deep and steady tones, hints of another land in the cadence.

Eleanor hastily tidied herself and put her needle through the next stitch needing execution. She also quietened her nerves as best she could.

'You are up still?'

He looked more relaxed then he had yesterday. The boots he wore now were Jacob's. She recognised the engraved silver buckles.

'I seldom retire before ten.' She gave this back to him and was glad when he came into the room and sat in the chair opposite.

'My brother said you went to Essex to the Bromworth estate?'

He nodded. 'Oliver leant me his carriage and driver. With such horses it was a quick run both there and back.'

'I hope it all went well.'

At that he laughed. 'Well for me and poorly for my uncle, but I am finally shot of Mr Aaron Bartlett and his plotting so at least now I will be able to afford my own boots.' He added this in a wry tone as he stretched his legs out before him.

'I heard that you had won a substantial sum at the card tables last night?'

He frowned. 'A dubious talent in the eyes of the *ton*. Once it was losing I was better at, failure more acceptable to the doyens of good taste here.'

She smiled because what he said was the truth. She had heard the rumblings of gossip before she had left Frederick's and the strong opinion on the Viscount's new ability to fleece any other man at the table was not flattering.

'Perhaps you should pretend sometimes to be a lesser player?'

He sat up at that and looked at her directly. 'Dromorne threatened to foreclose on his IOUs if I did not fully reimburse him last night.'

The truth of this made Eleanor place down her flowery craftwork. 'There was no choice for you, then?'

'None. Tonight, however, I have my title and my estate returned into my care. Undoubtedly there will be others who will come forward demanding payments of past debts that I have long since forgotten, but now I can manage.'

'You will open your town house again?'

'I have a man hiring staff as we speak.'

'And your memory? Has it been jogged

at all with the sojourn back to Bromworth Manor?'

'No. I had thought perhaps…' He let this tail off and shook his head. 'But, no.'

Standing, she walked across to the hearth, using the mantel for support. 'Then I want to offer you a proposition, Lord Bromley.'

She stressed his title. Better to make the suggestion formally and holding no whisper of emotion.

He looked up at that, his eyes darker than they normally appeared. 'A proposition, Lady Eleanor?'

'I want to help you retrieve your memory.'

After these words he said nothing, but merely waited.

'I was with you for many of the days that you have forgotten. The days before your attack,' she qualified.

'With me?'

She was not brave enough yet to give him all the truth. 'As a friend. You were at a loose end and so I accompanied you on day trips.'

The candles against the darkness, the smell of scented wax, his skin under moonlight, her unbound hair draped across the tanned folds of his shadowed arm.

She did not speak of this.

'Where did we go?'

'The Vauxhall Gardens. Hyde Park. Bullock's Museum. Fortnum and Mason. Gunter's Tea Shop.'

'Quite the potpourri of establishments.'

'There were others as well.'

'All in less than a week? Not a little acquaintance, then?'

She smiled and spoke with more trepidation than she meant to. 'The thing is, Lord Bromley, I might be able to help you to remember by going back.'

'Recall by association, you mean?'

'Memory aided by events that are familiar. I have been reading about amnesia. Hypnosis is one treatment, but so is the quieter option of passing again across what your soul would know and hence allowing a passage for the brain to reconnect.'

She recognised in her words the text she had studied all afternoon at Lackington's.

'Why would you do this? For me?'

'You are my brother's best friend and Jacob would be more than pleased to see your memory restored.'

He could not understand her motives. One thing was for certain—they were not quite as she had admitted them, for she had blushed bright red at his question and looked away.

What was it she was saying underneath her words?

'I truly went to Gunter's Tea Shop with you?'

That brought a smile into eyes that were anxious.

'Happily, my lord. You particularly enjoyed the chocolate sorbet in a pewter mould shaped as a pineapple. But then Gunter's frozen indulgences are all particularly alluring.'

He could not ever remember laughing with a woman as he did with Eleanor Huntingdon.

'I can see why that memory has been expunged from my recall, Lady Eleanor.'

'You brought a box of the extravagant pastries home. The almond croissant was your favourite.'

'To the Bromley town house?' Had she gone there with him, too? The tea shop was a place she might have accompanied him without being exposed to scandal, but to visit him at home?

As if she had said too much, she retreated into silence.

'Very well.' He gave this quietly as she looked across at him. 'Our first destination is the tea shop on Berkeley Square. I'll pick you up at two o'clock tomorrow and we shall go and have ice cream.'

'You are not staying here this evening?'

'My town house is being readied for me and it will be good to put my head down in a bed that I know.'

The sharp flash of anger that crossed into Eleanor Huntingdon's face as he said these words were another puzzlement.

'Then I look forward to tomorrow, Lord Bromley. On the last occasion you wore a dark blue jacket and beige trousers.'

'You think the details important?'

'I do.'

'What was it you had on?'

She frowned at that as though she could not exactly remember. 'It was warm so no doubt I had on one of my summer silks.'

'In gold?'

'Pardon?'

'I liked you in gold at Frederick's.'

'I am not certain I have…'

'Anything, Eleanor. Wear anything you feel comfortable in. I was teasing.'

A further blush at the informality of his using her Christian name. Jacob's sister was beginning to confound him completely and the thought crossed his mind that he would sit anywhere opposite her just to see her blue eyes smile. Even in Gunter's Tea Shop in Berkeley Square.

Had it been the same back then?

He could not ask her. He couldn't ask Jacob either. He swore under his breath because the loss of his memory was causing havoc in every sort of way possible and Eleanor's offer was the one avenue to help him get closer to finding out the truth.

He just hoped like hell that he had not hurt her.

She watched him leave and for just a second was transported back to the night before his disappearance. They had made love and it was late, but the magic between them seemed doused and awkward as he had escorted her to the front door of the Bromley town house and to the carriage that awaited outside.

He had not kissed her. She remembered that vividly. When she had reached up that last time he had pulled away, calling to his footman to escort her home, anger and distance in his voice. He had not even stayed to wave her goodbye either, the door shut firmly so that all light was gone. She had stumbled on the steps in the darkness and almost fallen.

Falling. It felt like that again now as uncertainty clawed at truth. She did not know him any more. The man she had imagined was different from the one he had become, but she was different, too, with the responsibility of Lucy. She was also scared of allowing him in once more and being hurt because of it.

The dry ache in her throat made her breath shallow.

Chapter Six

Nicholas spent the next morning in one of the more squalid parts of the Ratcliffe Highway, asking questions that might lead to answers about his uncle's involvement in his lost years.

Once he might have felt out of place in such a location but the forces that had shaped him in the Americas were the same as those he now trawled through in the pestilent dark alleys of Stepney. Destitution, filth, poverty and overcrowding abounded here and criminal activity was a direct result of that.

The smell of the river was everywhere and the toil of those who lived by it easily seen, the scavengers and mudlarks who survived on what they could find on the bottom of the Thames when the low tide washed in various pieces of coal, rope, bones or copper nails if you were lucky. Nicholas knew this because the James River had held the same desperation and there were times, especially in the early months there, when he had wondered about crawling into the sludge himself.

Those who held the run of the docklands were steeped in beggary and with no other means available to them were unlikely to overlook opportunities that might keep them from the workhouses.

Opportunities such as the kidnap of a viscount and his subsequent disposal. He'd had the name of a man who might have some information about such things, given to him quietly, of course, and taking the last of his gambling winnings from Frederick's soirée to obtain.

He'd dressed accordingly, but there must have been something in the lines of his face that spoke of menace and experience because walking through the mean streets of the place he had been completely unchallenged. Perhaps the scar did him a service here.

Mess with me and I will deal with you, as others have dealt with me.

The White Horse Tavern stood on the corner of East Smithfield and a smaller unnamed street, the river visible from its front portal. Those who watched him enter were miserably clad with barely a boot between them and the stench of the streets followed him inside to the bar where he recognised the look of some of the cheaper liquor he'd dispatched himself in Richmond.

A stranger approached then, a man in his forties with an eye that was patently false in its deformed socket, as well as being poorly fashioned.

'You'd be the one who has been asking about the details of a snatch in Jermyn Street some years ago?'

'I am.' Words were not things to be bandied by the starving in the same way as the *ton* was wont to. The less said the better.

'Join me over there.'

The very position of the man's seat told Nicholas two things. He liked his back to the wall and he felt safer near a further exit. A small door was visible beside the table, three steps running down to it.

The newcomer held his hand above his belt as he sat and Nick knew there would be a knife there. There was probably another one on the outside of his right boot given that was the side he favoured as he gestured to Nick to also sit.

'Did you bring money?'

'I did, but the amount depends on what you might tell me.'

Neither of them used names. The parish constables and the Night Watch were noticeable by their absence in these parts of London, but there were other means of maintaining order. Should the need arise for violence Nick knew the man would not hesitate and there were those close undoubtedly involved in the same scam. The lad in the corner tending to the fire, the bearded fellow behind the bar, the two older patrons to one side who were stiff with focus.

He turned back and waited, his breath quiet and even, but nevertheless relieved when the contact fumbled in his pocket to bring forth a small book.

Turning over the pages to find the right entry, the glass-eyed man read quickly.

22nd August 1812
Jermyn Street, Mayfair
Viscount Bromley
Twenty pounds
Paid

The shock of the words made Nicholas's breath come shallowly. 'Who paid?'

'An older fellow named Bartlett and an arrogant toff he was, too. The mark was put into a hackney coach and thrown into the river as per instructions and then left for the tide to take.'

Or to crawl out? To be picked up? To find a ship to faraway shores?

'Did Bartlett pay again later when it was discovered that the man was still alive? Did he have someone follow Viscount Bromley abroad?'

'No. That was the end of it. A simple drowning. No amount of gold would be enough to entice those I hire out to cross the seas to hunt further.'

'But others might?'

'I have never heard even a whisper of it, but I suppose with enough gold offered it could be possible.'

Nick believed what was said and the hope of a quick resolution wilted. His uncle might have ordered his demise in the first place at the river, but when that did not eventuate another had tried to finish him off.

He put a small bag of gold on the table, the clink of it satisfying. 'If you hear anything at all about this matter I would be well pleased to learn of it. Leave word at the address inside and mark it *"Stepney"*.'

As a duke, Jacob was often receiving missives. No one would take notice of a further messenger.

A quick nod of his head and the man stood, using the small door to disappear. There was mud on his boots from the river and his cloak was torn at the hem.

As Nick rose himself the tavern owner came forward and slugged him hard on the side of his good cheek.

'In warning not to say nothing of this to anyone.' He could feel the eyes of all the others upon him as he left.

She had worn the sprigged muslin to Gunter's six years ago, Eleanor thought as she rifled through the clothes she'd brought down to London from Millbrook House. But there was nothing here remotely similar to that which her eighteen-year-old flighty self would have once favoured. Certainly apart from the one very formal gown she had worn to Frederick's, there was nothing in gold.

Hauling out a deep blue velvet, she held it up against her. The colour made her eyes bluer and she had always liked the cut.

Sighing, she stroked her fingers across the pile. Was she doing the right thing? She

missed Lucy and every day she promised to
help Nicholas was one less she did not have
with her daughter. She wondered if she should
put more of a guard up, for her protection
and for Lucy's. But she wished his memories
back as desperately as he himself did because
only then she would know whether she could
trust him to be the sort of father her daughter needed.

The demons still sat upon his shoulders
and the menace that had become such a part
of him now was worrying. Still, yesterday
at Bromworth Manor he had discovered his
uncle's part in his mysterious disappearance
so that was one less concern. The debts he
owed should right themselves with his newly
come inheritance and things would return to
normal.

Normal?

He would never be the rakish pleasure-
seeking smiling Viscount she had once fallen
in love with, but her older self found this dangerous, larger and quieter version even more
attractive.

He was steel now, honed in fire, the pieces
that had been light and reckless burned away
to the bone. She could not even imagine how

this Nicholas might enjoy ice cream with her at Gunter's.

Despite everything she looked forward to their next meeting. It had been the middle of August last time they were there—now hot chocolate might be more the order of the day on a cold December afternoon. All she could feel was excitement.

His carriage arrived on the dot of two and Jacob called to her as she came downstairs hoping to leave before anyone saw exactly who she had gone with.

'Tell Nick to stop in for a drink here with me afterwards.'

Eleanor smiled because there was very little her brother ever missed when it concerned his family. 'I will.'

'And make sure he takes take good care of my baby sister.'

'Hardly that. I am almost twenty-five. A matron.'

He shook his head and stood. 'Experience does not always come with the years one lives, Ellie. I don't want you hurt.'

'You think I might be?'

'After all that Rose and I endured, I am now of the opinion that no one knows better what is right for your life than you do. But a word of warning. If you are hurt, let it be your making and not that of others. He is a good person, Nick, but in a difficult situation.'

'I know.'

'And you are a bit the same, I think.'

She made no answer to this as she turned to go, but sometimes she got the distinct impression that her brother could read her more easily than she gave him credit for.

Nicholas was just walking towards the town house after speaking with his driver and he looked up when he saw her.

'The while we keep a man waiting he reflects on his shortcomings.'

She frowned at his words.

'It's an old French proverb, though I have changed the pronoun.'

His explanation made her frown. 'What are your shortcomings then, my lord?'

'I have so many I cannot remember half of them.'

When he smiled she saw a dark bruise on his left cheek, newly gathered.

'I hope no one else has decided to try to do away with you since yesterday, Lord Bromley.'

All humour evaporated and when he didn't answer Eleanor felt a growing bud of alarm.

He was dressed in his own clothes this morning. A black jacket over lighter trousers, his white shirt and cravat enhancing the tan of his skin. His hair was back in a looser queue today, allowing wisps of dark brown to frame his face in a fashion that was unusual nowadays, but one that suited him completely.

Beautiful. She had always thought him that even in the very worst of times.

But this afternoon, as he helped her into the carriage, he felt less safe than he had yesterday. She could almost imagine he might scrap the plans for the tea-shop visit and head instead to find some frightening shadow-filled tavern in which to imbibe uncut liquor in great quantities.

For years she had lived so carefully, with circumspection and quietness. She had blended into Millbrook House without incident, making sojourns to London only occasionally and always being on her very best behaviour.

She had dressed appropriately, trying not to draw any attention to herself, she had spoken solely on topics that caused no debate and in any group she had always stood back rather than pushing herself forward. She had stayed well away from the masculine gender.

Camouflage. Penance. Lucy did not need a mother of any more notoriety or shame and Eleanor had done her level best to make certain that she was exactly the type of woman others expected.

She had grown old.

That thought had all her attention.

And staid.

Another shocking truth.

She had become a woman she would not have recognised at eighteen when she had thrown away all restraint and jumped head first into the thrall of Nicholas Bartlett.

'You seem preoccupied?' His voice came through all introspection and shattered her resolve with ease.

'Did you like yourself when you were younger, Lord Bromley?'

'Not much, I think, but responsibility and experience have weathered the rough edges.'

Given that she was thinking just the opposite, she smiled.

'I have always been careful.' She gave him this in reply. 'So careful that perhaps...' It was hard to finish.

'Offering to help me with my memory and coming with me to the places where I could find some recall is not so careful? There are

many here in society who would say I am a
risky man to know and stay well away because of it.'

'And are you? Risky, I mean?'

'My uncle would swear that I am and so
would those who hold debts from me which
have remained unpaid. Society always la-
belled me a wild cannon and my friends
might say it, too, because in the loss of self-
knowledge there is the propensity for chaos.
Sometimes in the late of night when I cannot sleep I may even admit it to myself. I am
damaged, Eleanor, and have been for a very
long time.'

'Even before you disappeared?'

He nodded, but she could not let the subject go so easily.

'A viscount who founded the most depraved
gentlemen's club ever to grace the hallowed
halls of Oxford University and then moved it
to Mayfair where it became even more dissolute and scandalous? That sort of damage?'

He shook his head.

'Every act within Vitium et Virtus has always been consensual. People are there because they want to be. No one is forced.'

'A morality within the scandalous?'

'Exactly.'

And right then and there Eleanor knew what she had missed the most when he had disappeared. It was this, this conversation that was more real to her than any other thing she had ever felt. Every single part of her was more alive in his company. Her body. Her brain. Her heart. Her soul.

He made her fascinating and brave and clever. Effortlessly.

'After meeting with a few people, I don't think my uncle was the one who paid people to follow me to the Americas.'

The bubble burst. Real life rushed in like a blast of frigid cold air, enemies poised again at every bend in the road.

'How could you know this?'

He didn't speak, but she could see the answer in his eyes, on his cheek and in the guarded quiet of his posture. He had not just waited for such information to trickle slowly down to him, but had gone to actively seek out the truth. Gone presumably into the poorest parts of London that few aristocrats would feel comfortable to be. Except him.

There was a certain respect in such an action that she could not help but feel. But to pretend joy and eat ice cream?

To laugh at the fussy decorative moulds

and sip at tastes inconsequential and unimportant when there was an enemy afoot who wished him harm in such magnitude?

She wanted to throw herself down on the plush leather seat of his carriage and sob because a day that had begun with such promise was now falling into complete disarray.

Damn it. He should not have said a thing about his suspicions. Now Eleanor Huntingdon was looking as though she might hurl herself out the window before the carriage stopped just to escape from his company.

He could not believe he had told her any of this. Usually he clammed up about affairs that were even remotely personal, but the laughter and ease of the conversation had been beguiling and he had let his guard slip.

There was no easy way to say that he was damaged and reduced in value, the spoiled and harmed product of years of fear and danger written inside him like a story. Any fineness he might once have had was diluted by experience, weakened by a lack of trust and diminished by an absence of honour.

Nick could still feel the stranger's neck in Shockoe Bottom breaking under his grip, the shameful truth of death by his own hand making him swallow down bile.

Like an apple in a barrel, rotten to the core. 'Please, God, do not let me hurt Eleanor. Please, God, keep her safe.'

He recited this beneath his breath as she turned away, the sky through the window about as bleak as his mood. He needed to throw off these maudlin thoughts, or she would decide to return home. There was probably only so much of him that even an angel like Eleanor Huntingdon could take.

The anger and shame reformed into effort.

'Would you like a walk first on the square before we go in for tea? We could stroll around the pathways. Is that something we did before?'

'No.' Her voice was hesitant.

'Good. Then let us make some new memories before remembering the other ones.'

Her coat and hat looked warm and her boots sturdy. A small walk in the cold might reinvigorate them both and shake the cobwebs from their worries.

He smiled because suddenly he remembered his mother saying that to him and when Eleanor caught his glance she tentatively smiled back. He wanted to make her laugh again and talk again, her truths revealing a woman who'd been saddened by life. He wanted them both to forget what had been and to concentrate on now.

He would ask Jacob more about her dead husband when they were alone next time and if he gave back flippant answers as he had before he would confront him further.

'Virginia was a place that winter took to with a vengeance,' he said as they exited the carriage and began to amble around the small neat square. 'But the coldest region I've ever been to was Caribou in northern Maine. It's close to Lower Canada where the air sets up in Hudson Bay and is sent southwards. If you happen to be in a river valley sleeping rough you'll know well sure by the morning that you should not have been there.'

'Were you? Sleeping rough, I mean.'

'For a good week. I was on one of the trails hunting at the end of autumn and had not expected it to turn to cold so quickly.'

'A different life, then. One you would never have had if…' She stopped and he liked her confusion.

'I was probably insufferable, the man you knew before?'

She laughed at that and gave back a query of her own. 'Why would you say that?'

'My gambling debts were rising and I could see no way out. That was one of the last things I remembered before I couldn't, arguing with my uncle about the sums I owed. Hardly auspicious.'

'I agree that you were reckless and wild, but there was something else there, too. Something honest. If there hadn't been I doubt I would have stayed around to bother.'

'Perhaps you were trying to save me even then?' He said this as a jest and she hit him lightly on the arm in return before she realised it was the injured one. Then he had to stop and listen to five more minutes of apology.

'You owe the world nothing, Eleanor, and remorse should always have its limits.' He could tell she was listening as she tipped her head. 'Regret is not an easy emotion to live by and if things do not turn out quite as you expect them to, then you need to shape your world to make sure that it does.'

'Do you do that?'

'I try to. Since coming home I try to forget what once was.'

'You have reshaped your life?'

The small line between her brows was

deep and because of this he gave her back something of his truths. 'Not entirely, but the pieces still lost to me will return. I know it.'

The tea shop on the south-east corner had now come into view and as expected it was half-empty, the cold driving the clients away. As they walked inside the man who met them asked if they had a preference for where they wanted to sit. Eleanor gestured to the table by the window.

'We sat here last time?' Nicholas said this as they were seated, the green and gold baize chairs small and dainty.

'A lucky thing it was, too, for a group had just moved off when we came and it was very busy. The summer view was better.'

'Yet Berkeley Square still holds its charm.'

He was careful with his words because so far none of this was in any way familiar.

'Tea for two, please.' She smiled at the waiter as she gave him back the menu.

'A simple choice. I was imagining the pineapple delicacy you told me about.'

'I was teasing you, Lord Bromley. We were only here briefly for we were en route to Bullock's Museum.'

'We shall go there tomorrow, then? I will pick you up at eleven.'

When she nodded Nick let out the breath he had not realised he was holding. Another outing. Further conversations. With the light from the window falling across her face he thought Eleanor Huntingdon was by far the most fascinating woman he had ever laid his eyes upon.

'We spoke of animals last time because there was a black spaniel sitting at that table there.' She gestured to a vacant setting over by the wall. 'You said you had had a dog most similar when you were young?'

The feeling of loss hit him so forcibly Nick thought he might have fallen off the chair had his hands not curled to the seat.

'I spoke of him?'

A frown marred her forehead. 'Are you remembering things? I think you said his name was Vic.'

The horror of what had happened to the animal made his heart beat quicken. Vic. Victor. Victory. His father had named him after the Siege of Bangalore in 1791. Another thought hit him like a sledgehammer.

'How close were we, Eleanor?' He'd never told another about the dog, its death one of the defining and terrible moments of his childhood.

* * *

Nicholas Bartlett looked at her directly as he asked his question; a question Eleanor had been expecting given the nature of her plan so she'd concocted exactly the right answer.

'We were friends.'

With a nod he looked away though she could see anger in the line of his jaw. It had been like that last time, too, but then he had been much less adept at hiding his sorrow. Now there was only the slightest hint of it. A man with his emotions well under control, the uncertainty of a few days ago gone entirely.

For a moment she could only stare at him, this harder, more unreadable stranger wrapped in the shape of the one she had lost her heart to, but then the tea came and the moment ran again into now as she thanked the waiter for bringing the refreshments.

Twinings black tea. The very same as last time.

Today though Nicholas Bartlett used his right hand to lift the cup. Then it had been his left. She noticed he still cradled the injured hand whenever he could. In the carriage it had lain against the top of his thigh, the swollen reddened fingers curled in pain.

She didn't want to ask of this though because she knew there would be some story attached to the wound that wouldn't be an easy one. Nothing about him at the moment seemed easy.

'We talked also of your hope of a Tory victory for the Duke of Portland in the next elections. You spoke on that for a long while.'

'A topic you must have found riveting?' The irony in his tone was obvious.

'You don't follow the turning wheels of government any more?'

'Not particularly. I think I am more in favour of living life quietly.'

'At Bromworth?'

He nodded. 'The land is fertile and the work is interesting. After so long spent moving from one place to another, I would like to find a base now, a home.'

When the waiter brought them milk Nicholas thanked him. Once he would not have noticed the ministrations of a servant at all.

'I live for a good part of the year at Millbrook House in Middlesex, my lord.'

'Why?'

'The life of a widow is a solitary one.'

'But you have your daughter? The child Jake told me of?'

'Indeed I do. Is this tea to your liking, for you enjoyed it last time?'

She did not wish to discuss Lucy with him and she hoped he had not noticed her leading him on to another topic.

'It is.' As he toyed with his cup she was reminded of the quiet a panther or a lion might employ before his next strike.

'Will you come to dinner at my town house, Eleanor?'

The shock of his invitation was startling. She wanted to tell him that this was not something they had done then, but that was a lie. She had gone alone to his town house and enjoyed a meal unlike any she could remember. A meal of anticipation and sensuality and climax that had been unequalled.

'As it would be my first foray into entertaining I would like to have friends there. I will ask Jake, of course, and his wife Rose.'

Friends. She felt an ache of disappointment and of sorrow.

'That would be lovely.' The very thought of an evening at the Bromley town house on Piccadilly actually made her feel like turning to run. There had been few servants there that evening six years before as the Viscount had given much of his staff the night off, but what if anyone left recognised her? What if his memory returned in the middle of the dinner? Her brother was a man sharp on detail and nuance and so was Rose. That was a further worry.

She was swapping one set of problems for another. She was walking on a tightrope much like the artists she had once seen perform in Astley's at the Royal Grove, but without the comfort of a safety net. Recreating their 'courtship' as closely as possible was turning out to be a lot more complicated than she had thought.

Could she know Nicholas Bartlett again? Would he ever let her in? Or had the years of apartness made them into people who were too different to rediscover the core of each other.

She felt her knee brush his thigh momentarily as he moved to change position, the touch sending fingers of shock through her whole body.

Breathless.

Absolute.

Gripping her fingers as hard as she could on her lap, she felt herself slip into the flame.

Lady Eleanor Huntingdon looked flushed. She was trying her hardest to appear normal, but her knuckles were white as she clenched her fists; the small blue artery in her throat beating at twice the usual rate.

His recent life had taught Nick to read the signs of high emotion in people and she looked more than agitated.

It was his dinner invitation. She had been flustered ever since he had issued it. Perhaps she was regretting her decision to help him and was wondering now how she could turn him down politely and leave him in this mire of non-memory?

As he finished his tea he saw the leaves in the bottom arranged in a pattern.

'Leaves like this can be read, I think,' he said, pleased when he saw that had caught her attention. 'Once a travelling woman in Richmond told my fortune from a pile of sticks she carried. I imagine it is the same principle for the leaves.'

The corner of her mouth turned up. 'What did she say?'

'She assured me that I would be rich, famous and more than happy, though she warned there was a valley of emptiness between me and my dreams. At the time, running from town to town without a clue as to who I was or why I was there, her words meant very little, but now...'

'Your memory. A valley of emptiness? I did not expect you to be one who would put much stock in the world of the occult?'

'Amnesia does that to one, Lady Eleanor. *"There are more things in heaven and Earth, Horatio, than are dreamt of in your philosophy."'*

When she laughed out loud the tension was replaced only by warmth.

'You used not to quote Shakespeare either, Lord Bromley.'

'Another difference, then, Lady Eleanor.'

'You remember nothing of this? Of Gunter's? Of the outing?'

He shook his head and wished it were otherwise.

The bells of St Martin's could be heard in the distance counting out the night hour of eleven o'clock. Rose snuggled into her husband's side in the ducal bed as the prevailing winds came in from the south-west, shaking the fragile glass panes with their force.

'Do you think Eleanor seems changed lately, Jacob? Happier, I mean?' She whispered this into his chest and liked the way his arm curled about her, holding her close.

'She went with Nicholas for an outing

today. To Gunter's. He came in his carriage and picked her up.'

Her smile came unbidden. 'The tea shop with all its fussy food is a place I can barely imagine Viscount Bromley being comfortable in.'

The shake of his chest told her that he had held the same thought.

'Perhaps my sister wants to help Nick become reacquainted with the ways of London life.'

'Like a small rabbit might aid a hungry fox, you mean?'

At that he turned, his eyes, pale in the fire flame, full of question. 'What are you saying, Rose?'

'Nicholas Bartlett gives the impression of such danger and distance that I would have imagined Eleanor to be running the other way and yet she is not. You said she has been lonely for such a very long time, but perhaps we might be hopeful for an ending to her solitude?'

Jacob laughed. 'Matchmaking is a precarious occupation, Rose.'

'I know, but they suit each other in a way that is surprising. At the ball when they danced I thought they looked completely right.'

'I doubt Nick would appreciate words on the subject from me, but I suppose a relationship could be possible.'

Rose ran her finger down across his cheek to his lips and then her touch fell lower. 'Which is exactly why we shall only watch from a distance, Jacob, but with hope in our hearts.'

He turned at that and pulled her down beneath him, his dark hair burnished by candlelight. 'You are both wise and beautiful, my love, and I thank God every day that he allowed us to find each other.'

'Show me,' she whispered and wrapped her nakedness about him. As he blew out the scented flame Rose had the distinct impression of strength tempered with gentleness, and the sheer beauty of Jacob Huntingdon, her husband, warmed her heart.

Chapter Seven

Eleanor found her grandmother in the library the next morning as she came down to breakfast.

'You look busy, Grandmama.' Her eyes fell to the large pile of books stacked in the middle of the table.

'That is because I am trying to understand the world that Nicholas Bartlett inhabited during his time away.'

Of all the things she had expected her slight and frail grandmother to say that was the very last of them.

'You have spoken with Viscount Bromley since he has been back?'

'Briefly. The first night he came home with Jacob I saw him in the hallway and he told me he had just returned from the Americas. His grandmother would have been saddened by his losses, I think, God bless her soul.'

'You knew his grandmother?'

'Anna Bartlett? Yes, she came out the same year that I did and I was glad that she died before her son and her daughter-in-law went. A terrible death and I was always glad that Jacob was Nicholas's friend when they both were sent up to Eton. You were his friend, too, if I remember rightly, Eleanor. That day in the Vauxhall Gardens just after you'd come out into society and I'd lost sight of you for a little while, I was certain he was there.'

'There?' Her heartbeat quickened.

'Watching the fireworks and speaking with you. He was always a beautiful child and he became a beautiful man even with his wild ways and a weakness for gambling. But then he was a boy. Now he is a man.'

Her words flowed around the alarm that Eleanor had felt ever since Nicholas's disappearance. Her grandmother was a woman who noticed things in a way others did not.

'I'd hoped perhaps...' She stopped, the crinkles at each eye deep.

'What? What did you hope?'

'That the happiness Anna always prayed

for would be bestowed upon him. Did you know Richmond is a town in Virginia, too, Eleanor? A beautiful place by the sounds of it.'

The juxtaposition of these words and Nicholas's at the tea shop made her head spin.

Once a travelling woman in Richmond told my fortune from a pile of sticks she carried.

How much of a conversation had her grandmother held with him?

'If he returns again, my love, could you ask him if he might come and see me and have a proper visit? I would like to chat further for old time's sake.' She took a breath and turned the page on a large atlas. 'You are looking lovely today, Granddaughter. It is a relief to see the fire back in your cheeks.'

Was it just coincidence, her grandmother's chatter, or was there some other purpose underneath her words?

The Huntingdon family sorrows had overshadowed joy for such a long time now: her mother's fatal illness, her own shame with an unmarried pregnancy and a lover whom she refused to name. The more recent deaths of her father and brother had been another blow and Jacob's tendency to blame himself for everything had left them struggling.

'I hope Lucy will be back in London in time for the New Year? I miss her chatter and her laughter.'

'She is due back here tomorrow, Grandmama, for Jacob and Rose have a small family party planned for the evening of the first of January.'

'And Nicholas Bartlett will be here, too?'

'I am not sure. Why?' These words broke through restraint and caution, and were harsh and discordant.

'Because it is simply nice when the parts of one's life come together, Eleanor. The old and the new. All the pieces of it finally making sense.'

'Sense?'

'There is a time for sadness and also one for joy. It is our turn as a family to find some happiness now and to look to the future. Had your father been here he would have been saying exactly the same thing.'

'I am glad I like you so much, Grandmama.'

Kissing her grandmother on the cheek before walking away, Eleanor recited the words of Ecclesiastes under her breath.

A time to weep and a time to laugh. A time to mourn and a time to dance.

She wondered which time it was now for her.

* * *

The place was as odd as she had remembered it, she thought, as she walked through the solid Egyptian doors of Bullock's Museum in Piccadilly. The inside was even stranger, large stuffed animals in a fenced-off enclosure and trees towering above that looked as if they came from some ancient and long-lost world.

Nicholas was waiting next to a glass case, glancing not at the artefacts but at the light that spilled in through the window above him. The sight caught at Eleanor with a poignancy that made her stop still and simply watch. He looked as out of place here as he had done at Gunter's, the danger in him only thinly veiled and a sense of carefully checked distance overlaying that. He had not seen her yet, one arm held against his chest as though it was painful, the opposite hand anchoring it.

Mr William Bullock's artefacts were many after a lifetime of travelling abroad and Eleanor wondered what Nicholas Bartlett's treasure trove might look like had he gathered small tributes from all his years in the Americas.

He seemed like a man who travelled light. Her brother had said he'd had one small leather case with him when he had come straight from the ship to the door of Vitium et Virtus on Boxing Day.

He had caught sight of her now, the wounded hand replaced at his side as he walked over. It shook slightly against his thigh.

'Surely this museum brings back some memories?' She said this when he stood next to her, hoping that humour might lighten the mood. 'The naked Hottentot Venus smoking a pipe and the Polish dwarf are not sights easily forgotten, after all. If anything were to jolt your memory, it might be them.'

He laughed at her words, all the lines on his face softening. 'Did you make me laugh like this before, Eleanor?'

The world around her stopped, just slowed down and stood still because there was a look in his eyes that she recognised. A hunger that made his dark eyes darker.

'I think that perhaps I did.'

He glanced away then, a frown deepening as he moved back a pace.

His lack of memory was more irritating today than it ever had been before because he knew suddenly he would have found Lady Eleanor Huntingdon as charming and fascinating six years ago as he did at this moment and he did not know what he had done about that fact.

Had he kissed her? Had he taken it further? That thought made him step away just so that he did not reach out because he could not trust himself as to what might happen next. The memory of the women he had bedded in the Americas also sat there in the equation. He was damaged goods. Eleanor deserved a man who was exemplary in every way, not one whose life had been marred irreparably in the messy business of surviving and who still did not know if he brought danger to those he had contact with.

He needed to keep things light to allow her an escape. A sign at the doorway gave him a subject.

'Napoleon's travelling carriage is here at the museum?'

The flare in her eyes dimmed at his query.

'The French General's personal belongings have been a very popular exhibition by all accounts, my lord.'

'A gamble that has paid off, then?' He was barely thinking of Bullock as he said these words and he had the impression that she might have known this. 'The risk of the un-known to fill one's heart's desire?'

'There is also a nightgown, a set of pistols, his boots and a cloak amongst other things. With the numbers who have come to view them it's said that Bullock has made a small personal fortune from the ticket sales. Many people have been speaking of it and I have only heard interest and fascination.'

Her words ran on, one over the other, giving an impression of nerves. He thought he had never met a woman who was more fasci-nating. They were passing tall cabinets now which were full of more of the sort of insects he had seen before in the front room.

'Your eyes are exactly the shade of that butterfly wing, Lady Eleanor. *"Morpho pa-leides".*' He read this slowly. 'One of the larg-est butterflies in the world apparently with wings of iridescent blue on one side and an ordinary brown on the other. It allows the in-sect the ability to disappear at will if you like. A camouflage against predators?'

The sort of disguise she used, he thought. At Frederick's soirée she had looked un-matched in a deep blue gown. Today she sported a coat of dull beige, an ugly hat jammed tightly over her head. Why?

'I have always been careful.' She had told him this in the carriage as they had made their way to Berkeley Square. *'So careful that perhaps...'* She had not finished.

So careful that perhaps life had passed her by? A beloved husband whom she pined for and a daughter who had kept her away from the London social scene? So careful that she saw him as only a risk?

'How old are you now, Eleanor?'

'Twenty-four. Almost twenty-five.'

She said it as if it were a great age and he smiled.

'Young then?'

'Sometimes I feel like I am a hundred.'

He swallowed because she kept doing this to him. Allowing him a small window into her soul that showed only a truth.

She had hurt him, she thought, in some way. Again. Perhaps her honesty was something he did not wish for. Perhaps in the aftermath of the lies he had lived with he now held a discomfort of the truth? Especially her truths, with all their corresponding sadness.

His hands were running across the door of Napoleon Bonaparte's carriage as if such a treasure was the only thing he wished to think about. Another couple lingering next to the conveyance watched him with interest and the man spoke suddenly.

'Bromley. My God, I had heard that you were back from the dead. David Wilshire.'

Nicholas looked at him for a second as if trying to place him. Finally he seemed able to. 'You knew Nash Bowles if I remember rightly and I beat you in a card game which you did not take kindly to?'

'I used to take losing more seriously than I do now,' the man said, 'though Bowles has not forgiven you. He still proclaims weekly that he is no friend of yours.'

'There are many more who might claim that honour, Mr Wilshire.' Nicholas's voice was tight, the tone in it hard.

'You are meaning those to whom you owe large debts at the gambling table, I suppose, though it is said now you are more proficient at winning than you once were.'

'Word travels fast in London. Did you also hear I suffer fools less gladly?'

Wilshire frowned and stepped back, tipping his hat in leave and dragging the woman he was with from the room. The Viscount looked after them with a frown.

'At school there were those students who

were bullies, cheats and troublemakers and he was one of them. I doubt he has changed.'

'Who is Nash Bowles?'

'A miscreant who wanted to be a partner in Vitium et Virtus in the early days and who was not pleased to be turned down.'

'By you all.'

'By me, in particular.'

Eleanor had the impression he was not telling the whole story, but she did not feel comfortable to press further, so she was surprised when he continued talking.

'Some of the men who hate me probably have good reason as there's only a certain amount of arrogance people can stomach before the bile begins to work.'

'People like Bowles?'

'No. Not him. His animosity comes from a whole different place altogether.'

There it was again, that uncompromising anger, that hard flash of steel in him that was so much different from the man he had been. But if she was truthful that same resoluteness was also a part of her character now. She and Nicholas Bartlett had been transformed in a way that was similar, hardened by life but still trying to live.

She liked the way he took her arm, after they exited Bullock's, and helped her across the road as they walked towards Green Park, though once on the other side he let her go.

'Did we walk much, then?' There was now decided interest in his words.

She wanted to say that they hadn't had time, particularly after the first few days when all they looked for were secluded and quiet areas to be alone together, to whisper and to touch.

To kiss for the first time in the back room at Lackington's when Nicholas had simply leaned over the dusty scientific tomes nobody ever looked at and taken her mouth beneath his.

A pure pain of shock ran through her at such a reminiscence. He had been slender then, softer. Just a youth. What would it be like to kiss this man he had become?

Could she risk taking him there tomorrow? To Lackington's? Part of her wanted to, but the other part felt only fear. What if he remembered and then scorned her? What if this new Nicholas wanted nothing to do with a woman who had thrown herself into his bed after only four days of knowing each other and had conceived an illegitimate child in the process?

'You seem quiet.'

'Oh, I am often that now, my lord.'

Love me, Nicholas, my love. Love me until we both die from the feeling.

She'd said that to him at the Bromley town house. Said other things, too, full of girly pathos and rampant exaggeration. She'd laid her heart on her sleeve and told him every little thought, every sorrow and hurt.

Now she could barely admit to anything because in the tiniest clue he might guess it all. Glancing across at him, she saw he looked full of thought, though he began to speak again after the short silence.

'For the first five weeks after I got to the Americas I lay in a poor house in Boston with fever until a reverend took me home and fattened up both my body and soul.' When he shrugged she could see the line of tension in his shoulders. 'That was the only time in all the six years I was away that I thought I was safe.'

She was astonished by such honesty.

'I tell you this because I am still not safe and that if you should wish to reconsider your kindness I will understand why.'

'My kindness?' She didn't quite know what he meant.

'Squiring me through these events that I have long forgotten. Truth be told, perhaps they are better left unremembered.' The flatness in his eyes was familiar and dragged at Eleanor's own protected sorrow.

'I used to think that after my mother died, my lord. I wished for no recall of her whatsoever because I had been hurt too much. Now, I struggle to remember her face, her voice, her smell and the irony is that I would give anything to have her visage back again.'

'Jake talked of her all the time at the club in the months after her death. You were lucky with such a mother.'

'How old were you when your own died?'

'Eight. Young enough to forget some things and old enough to remember others.'

'Seventeen was no better, I assure you.' She still remembered the shock and grief as if it were yesterday.

'My mother had hair exactly the colour of your own. In the sunshine there were threads of gold amongst the brown just like yours.' He smiled as he said this.

'I will take such words as a compliment, Lord Bromley.'

'Nicholas. Or Nick. And it was meant as one.'

There it was again, the difference in him

that she could not quite pin down. He was less evasive than he had been once and much more to the point. The flowery rhetoric of the past was well gone and in its place sat an honesty that was borne from adversity. She wished she might be brave enough to simply step forward and lay her hand upon his chest and tell him everything, but a vendor of hot chestnuts called out to them from further afield and her own sense of place and time was re-gathered.

'Are you hungry?' He looked altogether younger as he asked this of her. 'In New York they sold chestnuts, too, but they never tasted quite right. And now I know why. They are different from the ones here in England.'

Perhaps confessing past problems had been good for them both because she was starving and even from this distance the smell of the roasted nuts was delicious.

'Give me a moment, then.'

As he walked away to procure the treat another man coming through the park stopped before her. Swarthy and thickset, he had the look of a gentleman out of sorts with his world.

'You are Lady Eleanor Robertson, the Duke of Westmoor's sister, are you not?'

Flustered, Eleanor nodded.

'I was introduced to you once at a ball in

Chelsea and I seldom forget a face, particularly one as beautiful as your own.'

The slight lisp he had was as disconcerting as his words. She looked over towards Nicholas Bartlett, but his back was to her.

As the newcomer followed her glance, he, too, registered Lord Bromley's presence and the blood simply drained from his face to leave him decidedly pale.

'You are with Bartlett?'

Nodding, she looked away, certain that he must now move on and surprised when his hand covered her own.

'Gossip has it you are an experienced and generous woman and he is a cad and a spendthrift. If you would like to pass some time in my company, I am certain you would not regret it.'

Snatching back her hand, she stepped away. Was this person mentally sick? Could he hurt her? Should she run? Nicholas was back now and her first thought was that he had not waited to collect their chestnuts. Her second was more along the lines of amazement. He looked nothing at all like he usually did, the disdain in his face showing every feeling.

'Get away from her, Bowles.'

Nicholas's hand was in his pocket now and

Eleanor had the impression that he might have held a weapon there. In the mood he was in she was more than certain he would use it should this stranger be difficult.

The fury in Bowles was magnified as he spat out his words. 'Bromley. I had heard you were back, of course, but I scarcely believed it. Back from the dead like a cat with nine lives, though I have to say your appearance is altered for the worst. More contretemps in America? The result of your arrogance and your reckless testing of boundaries?'

'Stay away from me and from my friends. If you decide not to take this advice, then expect retribution.' Nicholas spoke quietly but there was a threat in every single syllable that was unmistakable, the echoes of an old hatred more than evident. He'd gained control of himself now, a stillness in him that was decidedly menacing and any emotions upon his face well hidden.

All fight seemed to go from Bowles and he turned on his heels and left them, the tap of his shoe plates distinct against the stones on the ground.

Nicholas bit back a curse. What the hell was Nash Bowles doing talking with Eleanor?

He didn't want that crawling amoral mongrel anywhere near her, his mind returning to the woman he'd found the bastard with in a back room of Vitium et Virtus just before he had disappeared all those years ago.

Nick had seen exactly what a madman was capable of then, the lines of carefully placed cuts on the girl's bottom weeping blood.

'It's a place of fantasy,' Bowles had shouted, his fists flying. 'And you have no business being in here and spoiling it. She's a serving maid, for God's sake, and will be well pleased with the trinket I shall leave with her as payment. Besides, the pleasure of pain is underrated.'

His victim's face told him exactly the opposite.

'Is that true?' As he'd asked the small dark girl this question she had simply shaken her head and burst into tears, trying to pull her clothes up to cover her shame in the process. There were more wounds on her fingers.

Without another thought Nicholas had picked up a much thinner Bowles by the scruff of his neck and thrown him out the front door, uncaring of his lack of dress and his plethora of threats. He fell in an untidy heap on to the pavement below.

'Never come back. If you do I will kill you slowly with as much pain as I can administer.'

'You will regret this, Bromley,' he had replied. 'See if you don't.'

Nick had laughed at that and lifting the small knife that the other had dropped threw it in an arc so that it landed within an inch of Nash Bowles's right hand.

'The only thing I might regret is not aiming that blade squarely into the space between your legs.'

That day long ago morphed into this one as Nicholas felt a warm hand tuck into the crook of his arm, his mind brought abruptly back from the past to the present.

The wind had risen and the grasses under the trees were being tossed in a silky blanket.

'I thought he might even have tried to drag me off with him.' Eleanor sounded breathless. 'I think he is deranged.'

'I am sorry. He won't hurt you.'

'He has hurt others?'

'Many, probably.'

'Then what is it he wants from you?'

'Revenge or the promise of silence? He is a bully and a coward and as he was interested in a stake of Vitium et Virtus for himself he was always hanging around the club.'

Her teeth were worrying her top lip. 'He would be a horrible person there, for there is something frightening about him, something broken.'

'You are right and I have first-hand knowledge that he does not truly comprehend the notion of a line between yes and no. He was an only child and more than spoilt so he imagines the world should be exactly as he should want it.' Nick breathed in deeply, trying to disperse the alarm he had felt when he saw Eleanor with Bowles. If she were to be hurt because of his past…?

'Will you play a part in the club's running now you are back?'

'No. I'm thinking of giving my share to the others if they want it.'

'I doubt Rose would like to see my brother more involved. The same might go for Georgiana and Cecilia.'

At that he laughed, the worry of the past few moments dwindling as he saw her smile. 'For a club steeped in secrecy there are now many who know the names of its founders.'

'Frederick's youngest brother keeps harping at them all for the chance of it, too. He is just finishing at university and is as wild as the rest of the chaotic and out-of-control

Challengers. You might consider him? He'd undoubtedly be perfect.'

As she moved closer it was as if everything in the world was better. He liked her near. He liked the way it felt when her thigh came into contact with his own as they walked across the grass.

He liked her questions and her truth. He liked how she had put all the facts of things together to come up with a portrait of now. He liked how she made him happy.

If he had Eleanor Huntingdon in his bed he would feel as if he could conquer the world.

He cursed under his breath and decided such invented fantasies might rival any thought up in the passion of the moment at Vitium et Virtus.

She felt him withdraw, just as he had done every other time they had come closer. Did he think she might deceive him in some way or harry him into making a decision he would come to regret.

Nash Bowles had riled him and yet it was more than that. Nicholas Bartlett's touch was tight as he took her arm and turned towards the road, chestnuts forgotten in his haste to be away. He also vibrated with an anger that was unfathomable.

'What did he do to you? This Bowles?'

He needed to talk so when silence was his only answer she kept on speaking.

'In the times that I thought the world was landing on my shoulders I realised confiding in someone trusted is often a helpful thing.'

His glance came around to her, wary and suspicious, full of the ghosts she could only guess at. The damage on his face today was so very easily seen in this light. She could imagine the force of the blade that had come down upon him and the pain he must have endured afterwards.

'Jacob was my confidant and he was a good one, too, because he mostly listened. As you are. To me, I mean. Listening.' Now she was flustered, his very presence warming her insides. It was confusing, this strength he had, this power to make her unsettled. She could not remember it before.

Finally, a smile curled at the end of his lips. 'I doubt some of my stories would allow you to sleep at night, Eleanor, were I to unburden myself of the past. You might be well pleased never to hear them.'

But she did not allow him that excuse.

'After being ill in the home of the Reverend in Boston, where did you go?'

'South.' The word was flat and quiet.

'Because you had to leave?'

'The Reverend had a daughter. A small child called Emily. When I was walking along the cliffs one day she followed me and was hurt.' He swallowed and she could see the strength of emotion in the grinding action of the muscles in his jaw. 'She was pushed,' he finally uttered.

'So you went south to protect them? To draw off the one who had pushed her. Was it the same man who hurt your arm and face?'

'I hope so because he is dead. I killed him.'

He looked at her directly as he said this, refusing to allow for misinterpretation, ensuring her understanding in a way he had not when they had talked during the waltz at Frederick Challenger's party. There was no line of apology or uncertainty anywhere. She could imagine a weapon in the ruined fingers of his left hand raised against evil. She hoped the death had been quick. Nicholas Bartlett was a warrior wrought from the softer bones of an English aristocrat. How different would he feel from each and every other coddled lord of the *ton*? A man who had been places

not one of them would have the misfortune to
venture or the endurance to see himself safe.
She could not quite leave it at that, though.

'Would he have killed you?'

'Pardon?'

'The man who hurt you. Would you have
been dead had you not fought back?'

He nodded.

'Then my opinion is that evil does not deserve to win out under any circumstance and
he warranted his fate.' Her words held that
certain conviction she heard herself use in
some of her dealings with her daughter. An
unequivocal truth. An unarguable logic.

She watched him run his hand carefully
through his hair, pushing the long and untidy
fringe from his face. 'I am glad, Eleanor, that
you have been safe here in England.'

Safe? Six years of the cutting words of others. Six years of pretence. Six years of lonely
isolation. Six years of carefulness tempered
by politeness and manners. She was so safe
she could scream with the cloying breathlessness of it. Better a cut like his to the very bone
and then an ending. Quick. Final. Though in
all honesty it seemed that the wolves might
still be circling.

A small summer house hidden amongst the

trees to the left of the path suddenly caught her attention. They had come here once in their effort to find quiet and out-of-the-way places and although the green shields of the summer trees were no longer in place the park was also far less peopled in winter than it had been back then.

'I want to show you something,' she said and was pleased when he followed her over the grass and came up the steps to the circular platform which sat above the Serpentine.

Greyness surrounded them. The sky. The water. The trees with their mottled winter bark.

Nicholas had to duck as he came beneath the boarding around the roof and she smiled at him even as she shivered with the cold.

'This whole winter has been freezing.'

She felt him there next to her, touching warmth along the length of their arms. A small intimacy in a large landscape and a connection that felt so right and true she made no attempt at all to pull away.

She was shaking.

He wanted to bring her full into his warmth, but he also did not wish to frighten her.

'I should have remembered the chestnuts,'

he said and liked the way she laughed. 'But I do have this.'

Pulling his flask from a pocket, he screwed open the top. 'It will warm you up at least.'

When she took it she sniffed at the top of it in a way that told him she did not quite trust what was inside.

'Is it strong?'

Before he could answer she took a swallow and began to cough, the purity of the liquor making her hand the flask back.

'Scottish whisky and the best my uncle could buy.'

'I have heard it said that Aaron Bartlett has left the country having taken money from the Bromley coffers.'

'In truth I don't care what he took, it's only good to be rid of him. Bromworth Manor is being cleaned of his presence, just as the town house was, and soon there will be nothing left of his legacy there at all. His son has followed him by all accounts so there is another worry gone.'

He tried to keep the bitterness from his words, but did not think he had succeeded when Eleanor looked at him with sorrow in her big blue eyes.

'How was your guardian related to you?'

'He was my father's brother and I hated him right from the start. He was never a kind man or a good one and young children, for all their innocence, easily recognise duplicity when confronted with it.'

There it was again, a truth he had given to very few others. His hand tightened on the wooden handrail that he leant upon, but he liked how her warmth fastened him to goodness and hope. An anchor to a world he had been gone from for so long.

With Eleanor the shadows lightened and the demons that rode on his shoulders daily were less heavy. Frowning at his flowery thoughts, he scuffed at a broken baton at his feet.

'Do you have any family left now? Anyone at all?' She looked stricken as she asked her question.

'None.' The word was bare of emotion. He no longer craved the tie of blood as he once had as a child and even as a youth.

'You could share mine, then. Grandmama is most adamant that she needs to keep an eye on you and you have always been Jacob's best friend.'

The sweetness of her offer astonished Nick, though he did wonder where she herself stood on the spectrum. He suddenly wanted to kiss her, to bring her into his arms and take her mouth in a hard stamp of ownership and possession. The feeling was so strong he turned and moved away, a flurry of freezing cold wind and rain aiding his want to escape.

'Come, Eleanor, I think I should take you home.'

Chapter Eight

⁓⁓⁓

The town house was cloying. Nick thought that as he wandered the environs of his library later that same day, picking up this and that as he went.

A racing broadsheet. A book on sexual positions from the East. A lewd statue of the female form made of ebony. He truly could not remember buying this even with the return of his memory. Had he actually paid money for such a thing and liked it?

His servants had emptied the rooms of his uncle's possessions and taken out all the objects that Aaron Bartlett had brought into the house.

What was left was surprisingly meagre. There were barely any books to read and the numerous gambling dices, cards and tokens lying on various shelves reminded him exactly where his interest in life had mostly lain.

And he had been so bad at it, too. To put all that effort into something that he had so little aptitude for amazed him.

A small bracelet plaited of coloured thread inside a box on the mantel held his attention because it was so out of place. Why would this be here? He measured the strands against his own wrist and worked out it must have been the possession of a female he had known. This puzzled him more than anything.

His taste in women had been eclectic and varied, but he had usually escorted well-connected young ladies of the *ton* or the high-flying courtesans from Vitium et Virtus. All these ladies he knew preferred diamonds.

Lifting the small circle to his nose, he took in breath. A faint smell of violets. A wave of heat hit him forcibly. Lady Eleanor Huntingdon?

Nothing made sense and yet everything did. He could feel her here through the fog, laughing at him, egging him on, sitting with him before the fire, her hands firmly entwined in his own.

Was this a hope or a reality? He could not grasp the essence of it and his damned headache was worsening just as it always seemed to when he tried to force memory.

Voices outside had him turning, the small plaited bracelet tucked carefully into his trousers pocket.

'Mr Gregory, sir.'

Oliver came in, a broad smile on his face.

'I missed you at Fred's the other night, Nick, and thought perhaps we could catch up now for a drink. I also brought back a book you'd leant me just before you disappeared.'

Defoe's *Robinson Crusoe* was in his hands, the burgundy-leather cover familiar.

'At least I had one tome in my possession that was worth reading. I remember this.'

'So the whole of your memory is back?'

'Not quite all of it.'

'Jake said you are certain it was not your uncle who had followed you to America and that you had been out looking for clues as to who else held a motive. Is that where you got the bruise on your cheek?'

Oliver had always been the one to notice if things were not quite as they should be. 'Bartlett didn't send anyone overseas. I know that much, though he did mean to drown me in the Thames. He is a man of small vision like his son. I doubt if he could have come up with a plan that encompassed searching for me across years and oceans. If I can remember the last week before I disappeared, then perhaps I might remember other men…'

'I saw you on one of those days with Jacob's sister outside Fortnum and Mason's in Piccadilly. She might have some ideas to help you.'

'She is already.'

'Is what?'

'Helping me retrace the moments.'

'Does Jake know of this?'

'I'm not hiding anything.'

Oliver frowned. 'Eleanor was broken completely when she returned from the Highlands.'

'I thought she had resided in Edinburgh.'

'No. Her husband was some sort of a northern laird up by the western coast. He was drowned apparently in a boating accident in the autumn a year or so after you left and Eleanor returned home to Millbrook House. She has a young daughter so we do not see her much in London now, which is a shame. There was also some talk that she never married the fellow at all though Jacob soon put paid to such gossip.'

Such a varying account floored Nicholas, for it was nothing at all like the facts Frederick had regaled him with. All this supposition was quite patently hearsay and Nick wondered at the true story. Still, if Jacob had not told Frederick or Oliver of it he doubted it would suddenly be related to him.

But why the secrecy?

His hand slipped into his right pocket and he felt the threads of the bracelet and its beads beneath the pads of his fingers. Tomorrow he was taking Eleanor to Lackington, Allen & Co. in Finsbury Square and he'd always liked the look of the façade of the place. She'd seemed tense when he had asked her of their next destination and he had wondered if anything had happened there between them to make her feel this way.

Oliver raised his glass towards him as he took a seat on the leather sofa by the windows.

'Here's to your return and to the future.' His smile was wide and honest. 'You were my first true friend here in England and it's good to have you back.'

'It's good to be here, Oliver.'

'God, Nick, I was such a green boy back then, wasn't I? One day at a new school and they were already teasing me about my Indian background and the colour of my skin and of the different way I spoke, until you showed up.'

'With my ire up and fists flying. I'd been practising my boxing skills at Bromworth Manor that summer holiday if I remember correctly and wanted to put them into practice.'

Oliver shook his head. 'It was much more than that, I would say. There were two of us and ten of them and you had a split lip and a black eye for weeks after and a broken wrist to boot. But they never bothered me again.' He twirled the crystal stem of his wineglass in hand before glancing up. 'I used to think of that after you had gone and for years I combed the city for you and paid agents to try and understand what had happened in the back alley of Vitium et Virtus. Even when people said that there was no hope left I always held out for some...' He stopped and took a drink. 'So here is to our friendship, Nick, and to brotherhood and to finding the bastard who did this to you. We are all in this you know. We all have your back.'

'I do know and I thank you for it and when I have need of help I will let you know. Coming back again has been a revelation, all the differences and the changes. I have never seen you look quite so happy. Where did you meet Cecilia?'

Oliver stretched his long legs out before him as he took his time to answer. 'In Paris. She was at the time employed in a gentlemen's club and went under the name of Madame Coquette. She was quite famous.' The laughter in his eyes made it known the story was not exactly as he said it.

Nick drank deeply before answering, 'Here's to women who are not boring, then, and who know how to please a man.'

'Oh, a good woman is much more than that, Nicholas. To be with someone you love is about the warmth of friendship and the certainty of a future. There's a comfort, too, in the complete absence of lies and after living a life like mine that is more than a relief.'

'By the sound of things you have all found women with as many secrets as your own. Perhaps that is the trick of happiness?'

'I think fate plays a hand, too, and timing.'

'I'll drink to that.' But all Nick could think of as he smiled was the lost week that Eleanor Huntingdon was doing her best to try to make him remember.

'Eleanor Huntingdon is helping Nicholas retrieve his memory.' Oliver said this to Cecilia when he returned home for she was waiting up for him in the morning room.

'Is he recalling anything else leading up to his disappearance?'

'Seems he is not, but Jake's sister is squiring him around town, trying her hardest to facilitate his memory.'

'Were they close? Before this happened, I mean?'

'I can't remember. I didn't think so, but…'

'I hear all sorts of accounts of Lord Bromley wherever I go. He was somewhat wild, I gather, and seldom seen out of the company of women.'

'He was lonely. Like me.' Pulling her from the wing chair, he sat down himself and settled her on his lap. 'You are warm and comfortable, my love.'

She laughed at that. 'Like an old slipper?'

'Warm and comfortable and sensual as hell,' he amended and kissed her.

'That's better.' She leaned back against him, her rich brown hair released from its pins and clips burnished in the firelight. 'Eleanor Huntingdon is strong and sensible and I have liked her a lot each time I have met her. She is not a lightweight woman, yet she holds secrets and they worry her.'

'Such intuition is not to be trifled with. I concur with your conclusions.'

'Perhaps Nick is the man to help her, then? The way you speak of him, Oliver, gives me the impression that he was never afraid of anything.'

'The attraction of opposites, you mean?'

'Well, if he was reckless and dissolute you also said that he wasn't a man who was unfair. And if he is lonely…?'

'Perhaps they might find solace in one another?'

He was now laughing so much he could barely kiss her although he tried. 'Are you by any chance lending your hand to that dubious art of matchmaking, sweetheart?'

'If I invited them for afternoon tea, would you promise to be circumspect, Oliver? We could then test the waters, so to speak.'

'Let's go to bed right now and I will show you just how circumspect I can be.'

Oliver lifted her up then and their reflection caught in the window, light against dark, and he wondered anew as to how he had been lucky enough to find such contentment.

Happy chance and good fortune. The two blessings had been largely missing in his life before he had met Cecilia. He hoped with all his heart that Nick might finally find the same.

After Oliver left Nick retired to his bed-chamber, the blues on the walls restful and mellow. He'd loved this room and coming in here as a young boy to curl up on the enormous bed with his parents and talk.

The same slice of regret ran over him, far more remote than it had once been, but still there none the less. Their deaths were the point where his life had begun to spin out of control, a wildness growing that became unchecked and complete.

The clock on the mantel chimed one. It was late and yet the night felt alive. With ideas and thoughts and hopes.

Cecilia was pregnant. Oliver had told Nicholas that under the threat of confidentiality. A new life. Another generation and the responsibility of guiding and teaching a child about what it was to live well.

As Eleanor had taught her daughter?

'Lucy.' He said the name out loud, liking the sound of it. A little girl. He wondered if she looked like her mother. He hoped she had Eleanor Huntingdon's vivid blue eyes and brave spirit.

His glance fell on the piano in the far corner of the room and he walked over to pull out the seat. He had not played in years and he wondered why the instrument had been left here in this room when piano playing was so much outside his uncle's endeavour or intention.

Setting his fingers above the keys, he began to beat out the *Moonlight Sonata* by Beethoven. He recalled so much more of his early years when he played. That's why he had stopped in the first place, he supposed, out of pure sorrow. It was also why he could never quite abandon it.

He did not know when he'd started thinking about the music instead of hearing the notes. It was after his parents had died and he'd returned in the holidays to the cold unwelcoming Bromworth Manor. It was in loneliness that he'd gained the nuances of the pedal and had started to notice that silences, too, could be shaped by emotion.

He did this now even after all these years of awayness. He rode the edge of the beauty between easy and hard, and was absorbed in the sweet and powerful truth of the notes.

He'd never played for anyone, not even Jacob or Frederick or Oliver. He doubted they even knew he could hold down a tune. No, the music was his alone, his and his parents. A connection. Him on one side and them on the other. After his conversation with Eleanor today such a realisation was enlightening.

Lack of sleep made Nick feel wary though in those brief moments it had found him, his dreams had been strange amorphous ones full of ghosts and dead people.

It was the piano, he supposed, and the music that had wrapped around his regret and brought his parents closer. Jacob's older brother Ralph had been there, too, with surprise on his visage at his newfound demise, blood still at his temple. The world they inhabited had been full of clouds and mist and fireworks.

That thought brought a frown because his mother had always hated the noise of them.

Eleanor was waiting for him outside Lackington, Allen & Co., a blue bonnet tied firmly under her chin and in a coat the colour of a churning winter ocean. He thought for a moment she had never looked more beautiful or more vulnerable.

'You are early?' He said the words as a question, stopping himself from reaching out and taking her hand again. It was a good ten minutes before the hour she had allotted as their meeting point yesterday.

'Last time I was early, too.'

She did not look at him directly as she said this, her glance sliding away and a hitch in her voice. The façade of the Temple of the Muses was shining, whether from the recent rains or from the lightness of the clouds he could not tell.

'You once told me that you had bought the book *Robinson Crusoe* from here and read it in a day.' She said this as they walked up the stairs into the main room with its imposing galleried dome.

'One of the few I ever purchased, then, according to the state of my library.' He liked her soft laughter. 'Actually Oliver Gregory returned the Defoe copy to me last night when he dropped in for a drink. He also said he'd seen us outside Fortnum and Mason a few days before I disappeared. What was it we were doing there?'

'Buying wine as a celebration.'

'What were we celebrating?'

'I can't really remember.' Her cheeks flamed and the memory of something was so firmly written on her face that Nick knew she lied.

* * *

The wine was a celebration of our first kiss here at Lackington, Allen & Co. at Finsbury Square.

It had been summer and the day had been hot and so they had gone to find chilled wine and a small hamper of food for a picnic by the Serpentine.

Then, he had looked at her as if she was the most beautiful woman he could imagine. Now he only appeared perplexed. At her poorly formed falsity probably and her reddened cheeks. She had not blushed in six years and now she was doing so on an hourly basis.

Well, it had to stop. She was no longer eighteen and foolish and Nicholas Bartlett was hardly going to take her hand and run laughing through the streets in search of sweet treats and then kiss the dusted sugar off each finger as she ate them.

The sheer absurdity of it made her smile.

She noticed that everyone watched him, covertly, his sheer presence now impossible to miss. At six foot two he had to bend at the portal, yet he filled the room with such a masculine grace and power that it took her breath away.

'I visit the library every time I come down from Millbrook House to London.'

'And is that often?'

'As little as I can possibly manage it, truth be told. Usually only at Christmas.'

'The life of a widow is a quiet one, then? Tell me, where did your husband hail from?'

'Scotland.'

'Fred Challenger says he was from Edinburgh and Oliver Gregory swears it was the Highlands. There is a difference?'

She felt suddenly sick and a sheen of sweat built on her top lip. 'You have been asking about me?' He was a man who could discover facts about her past that few others could. If he put the timings of her return together and the birth of Lucy...

'Only in passing, but I am sorry for your tragedy, Eleanor. It must have been hard to be so alone.'

'I have my daughter.'

'And I am glad of it.'

He did not patronise her or give unwanted advice. He spoke only in words that were simple and true.

It must have been hard to be so alone.

Because he had been lonely, too, she thought. In childhood on the death of his parents and in the wild dangerous antics of his youth. In the card rooms of London when the numbers never added up and he was left with a handful of debtors shouting for payment and an uncle who was withholding his inheritance. Certainly in his restless years abroad when he had shifted from place to place with an unknown killer on his tail and a memory that gave him no recall of peril.

Even here now, in the over-stacked salons of Lackington's, he looked unapproachable and out of place.

For a second she wondered if she had the heart to climb the steps to the small scientific reading room they had visited last time and find the quiet spot at the end of a row of shelves. Could it ever be again like it was, that young unbridled love, breathless with passion? Giddy with the thrall?

Now she was shy of him in a way she had not once been for she'd seen the glances every woman had thrown his way no matter where they went. Desire had that certain raw and hungry look she hoped could not be discerned on her own face.

'Penny for your thoughts, Eleanor?'

She smiled at his question and gestured to him to follow her.

Every leather-bound tome looked as if it had not been touched for years, the dust settled in the interim. The view was a fine one, however, and he went to the window to peer over London.

'When I arrived here I thought everything looked so neat. The houses, the streets, the people.'

'America is more wild, I suppose. Less ordered.'

'It is in parts, but there is a sort of beauty in that. Perhaps it was the same for you in Scotland?'

'Scotland?'

'Where you lived with your husband?'

'Oh, yes, it was.'

Digging into his pocket, he felt the small plaited bracelet and brought it out on his palm to show her.

'Is this yours, Eleanor? I found it in a wooden box on the mantelpiece in my library.'

She began crying just like that, one moment shocked and the next inconsolable, large tears running down her cheeks even as her hands came to wipe them away.

Crossing the room, he took her in his arms and liked how her head fitted exactly beneath his chin, the warmth and softness of her astonishingly right. She smelt of violets and freshness. He knew the moment she gained control because she stiffened and pulled away.

'I am sorry.'

He noticed that she held the colourful circle of thread tightly in her fist as though she might never let it go.

'It is valuable?'

'To me? Yes.'

Eleanor could feel her bottom lip still quivering and knew her eyes were red. When he gave her his kerchief she blew into it and then began to worry because she did not quite know whether to hand it back to him or tuck it into her sleeve to wash later.

These huge swings of emotion were something she had not felt with Nicholas six years ago in the happy haze of their new love. Then it had been easy and light.

Now everything weighed heavily upon them. Their past and their future and the present, too, because there was a danger close that she could not quite decipher.

She had given him her bracelet after he had made love to her. A circle of threads plaited for her by her mother from her tapestry basket and beaded at the end in the colours of primrose, green, cerulean-blue and *coquelicot*-red. When she'd explained how important it was he had held the gift and looked as though she had given him the world.

Today the limp gaudy bracelet had appeared tired and out of place between his thumb and forefinger, fingers that gave no impression at all of being that of a cosseted lord. There were small thin white scars across his knuckles now.

The hand of a fighter, the hand of one who had endured much hardship. A tougher hand altogether.

And yet when he had held her in his arms a few minutes ago all those elements of danger, menace, toughness and peril had only made her feel safe.

'I did not sleep well last night, my lord, and I am sorry for such an outburst.' She felt she needed to explain.

'Did I give you anything back in return?'

'Pardon?'

'When you gave me the bracelet, did I find something of mine for you?'

Another kiss. She nearly said it.

Instead she shook her head and simply looked at him, at the small gold chips at the outer edges of his brown eyes, at the wound on his cheek which today seemed lessened and a part of him, another way of how his time in the Americas had been imprinted into now.

He was even more handsome than he had been, the hard and thinner planes of his face melding into high cheekbones and a strong chin. Not in the manner of the Greek gods, unmarred and perfect, but following in the fashion of a Norse one, scarred by battle and war and the fighting arts held dear by the Viking marauders.

He could protect Lucy and her. From everything.

He had kissed her right here last time in the slant of sunbeams coming in from the window. He had taken her hand and pulled her into him, slowly, never looking away, and with his fingers in the nape of her hair his mouth had come down upon her own, allowing no escape as he had deepened the connection and taken her heart.

Unforgettable.

Eleanor stood there in the dim winter light and wished with everything she had that he might remember.

Something had happened here in this room last time. He could see the shadow of it in eyes remote with memory. He touched her lightly.

'The scent in the bracelet is violets. Your scent. Why did you give it to me?'

'You had told me of how you had lost your parents and I wished to make you happy again.'

'My parents?'

'You said you played the piano sometimes to remember them. You said you felt them close just there on the other side of the music.'

Shock tore through his equilibrium.

'You said sometimes when you could not sleep you played the *Moonlight Sonata* by Ludwig van Beethoven to try and reach them and you felt you did.'

His sudden loud curse shocked her.

'Are you ill?' Worry clawed into her words as he held on to the table, his knuckles white.

'It's just a headache. The same one I have had ever since...' He stopped.

His emotions since the incident at Richmond had been more distant than he remembered them. But now the sharp edges of feeling returned forcibly and all he wanted to be was alone.

At the Bromley town house an hour later he poured himself a stiff whisky. He could not work out what was happening, for the threads of the conversation between himself and Eleanor were as entwined and complicated as the pattern in the bracelet. Triple stranded and double braided.

Why should he have told her of his secrets when he had not even confided in Jacob, Oliver or Frederick?

The answer, of course, was simple.

He had known her far better than she'd ever admitted, not just as her brother's friend, as she'd said, but as something more important. He'd hurried her home to Chelsea from Lackington's with all the speed of someone on the verge of a collapse.

He swore roundly and hated the shake in his hands. He'd been an irresponsible and pleasure-seeking youth, distracted by both gambling and women. He could not even imagine how the Eleanor he knew now might have tolerated such weaknesses.

He hoped she had not known of his mounting debts and of the ugly characters from London's underbelly who had frequently come knocking at his door. He prayed he had not tried to sleep with her.

Jacob's voice interrupted his reveries.

'Good to find you home, Nick, because a

message came for you this morning and the one who delivered it said it was urgent. A poorly dressed man by the sounds of it and a fellow who my butler said he would not like to meet in the darkness? A colleague of yours?'

'Have a drink, Jake.'

He was glad when his friend sat down.

'Remember I told you of my uncle's involvement in my disappearance? Well, the information on the payment to those who cornered me in the alley behind Vitium et Virtus came from a man in a tavern in the docklands. He runs a protection racket, but seems to have extended his area of business into the art of kidnapping for a generous sum of money.'

'And Aaron Bartlett paid it?'

'He did. He'd had designs on my title and inheritance since the beginning and given the scandals surrounding the club he used his chance to have me gone.'

'And this new message?'

'I asked the ringmaster to put his ear to the ground to see whether he could find any trace of those who had followed me to the Americas. He was certain it was someone different from my uncle, someone with a lot more money.'

'And you think he has found this person?' Jacob handed over the sheet of paper sealed with wax.

When Nicholas broke it open he read out the message. 'Perhaps. He wants to see me again this evening.'

'I will come with you.'

'No. He will only meet me.'

'So you are still hell bent on doing this alone?'

'For now, Jacob. Until I need help.'

'Very well, but Eleanor said you were feeling unwell at Lackington's. She looked worried. She also said that none of your lost memories seem to have returned.'

'Did she say anything else?'

'No. Should she have? It's good that she's helping you. She is lonely and has lived a long time under the cloud of widowhood.'

'Where did she meet her husband?'

'I think you should ask her that.'

'Oliver said he lived in the Highlands and Fred was adamant Edinburgh was his abode.'

'They don't know anything about her marriage.'

'It seems nobody does. When was Lucy born?'

'After Lucy's father died. She was born at Millbrook House.'

'I see.' He felt a pang of sadness that the small daughter was not his.

'If you hurt Ellie, Nick, I will make you regret it. She's been hurt enough already. But I did not come here to issue threats. Tomorrow is New Year's Day and I have come with an invitation to a small family gathering. Lucy, Eleanor's daughter, has arrived from Millbrook and I am certain you will enjoy meeting her. Grandmama especially has impressed it again and again upon me that she would very much like you there. Your grandmother, by all accounts, was a good friend of hers and as such she feels some responsibility in ensuring your happiness.'

Family. In the light of his conversation on the topic with Eleanor that thought had him swallowing the rest of his brandy.

'Thank you. I should like to come.' As he gave his acceptance he was taken by the idea that for a moment Jacob looked worried.

Chapter Nine

The tavern was darker than last time, the weather dull and ominous. He'd brought his knife with him tucked into his right boot just in case. The sling he'd discarded because it didn't pay to show the slightest bit of vulnerability in places like this one.

He knew that to the core of his being.

The ringmaster did not appear to be present yet, but that did not faze Nicholas. Ordering a drink as he came in the door, he strode over to sit at the same table as last time, making sure to leave the seat against the wall free.

His ale arrived, the barkeeper who had given him the bruised cheek last time looking belligerent.

'He'll be here soon.'

Nick did not answer.

Over in one corner a group of four men

were playing cards. In the other a single occupant appeared to be almost asleep over his glass.

Such careful acts of staging were not new to him. For a while in the Americas before he perfected his methods at cards he'd used his other skill: his fists. It had been many a man he had thrown drunk from the tavern where he worked when they failed to see his role in the keeping of order by noticing all the small signs of discontent.

After ten or so moments the little door to the left opened.

'Do you have the payment?' The glass eye of the ringmaster glittered from the small light at the door.

'It depends what you've brought to show me.'

As the man sat he placed a card on the table.

'Vitium et Virtus.'

'What is this?'

'It's the name he paid with, a well-spoken lord who set the mark on Viscount Bromley over the seas. A goodly sum, too, it was, by the accounts of my source, and all in gold. I keep every bit of paper clients give me, just to be safe, you understand. Toffs believe people like me to be reckless and illiterate, but I was never that. I make careful notes of people and keep tight records. They come in handy sometimes.'

'Like now?'

The silence between them settled until the other broke it.

'I imagine that you have many enemies, to do a job that brings you out to places such as these ones.'

When Nick nodded, he continued on. 'Perhaps you believed in something once. Believed enough for others to want you hurt for it and now vengeance drives you?'

Such a warning from a street philosopher was all the more surprising because it was true. He had believed in Vitium et Virtus because it was like the home he had never had, a place away from his uncle and with as few rules as he wanted. A place where he could lose himself in fine wine, good women and high-stakes gambling, and be happy for a fleeting moment. Should he begin there in his search?

The well-spoken lord who set the mark on you. The sum was paid in gold. More clues. Someone of his own social standing, then? The ringmaster would not know of his own title for Nick had disguised his voice each time they met and worn clothes that fitted exactly into the setting of the docks. Here he was believed to be a thief-taker operating in the shadowy world between criminals and the law and caught in its complicated web.

With care he extracted his coins and placed them on the table.

'We will not meet again, I think,' the other said, 'but I wish you luck.'

The money was gone in the blink of an eye and as the barman crossed the floor to collect the empty glass Nick's fingers settled on the shaft of his knife.

Glancing down, the man cocked his head.

'We don't kill our own,' he said, leaving Nicholas to wonder just who he had become in the eyes of these thieves.

He wandered the river on the way home, mindful of those who watched him, but not afraid. This sort of place had been his home, too, once and the dirt and the smell of it was almost comfortable. Before the Americas the man he was would have been fearful to venture anywhere near such poverty.

He would call a meeting between Jacob, Frederick and Oliver and between them they could try to think just who the perpetrator could be. It was time he was honest with them and time to ask for their help.

The youngest Challenger was waiting at the Bromley town house when he returned, scrambling up from the seat his butler had assigned him in the library. He was dressed well.

'I am sorry, sir,' he said as Nick walked in. 'I am Frederick's brother Christian Challenger. I should have perhaps come back another time, but there is an important matter I wish to discuss with you and so I elected to wait.'

When his eyes saw the workman's clothing Nick was wearing they widened. 'There are so many stories of who you are now, Lord Bromley, and how you walk in the East End of London without fear and often in disguise. You are a legend, sir, to all of those young men who come after you. No one ever truly knew quite who you were then or are now and if we could be half the man that you—'

Nick interrupted him. 'What's the important matter?'

'Vitium et Virtus. Myself and a group of friends are wondering if perhaps you might sell your share in it to us.'

'Why?'

That question made Christian Challenger frown and yet to give him his due he answered.

'We'd like the chance to continue the club in the august tradition of friendship that you began, sir.'

A good retort. Perhaps Frederick himself had tutored the young man in an appropriate response. God, Nick suddenly felt every one of his twenty-nine years.

'When do you require an answer?'

'Oh, there is no hurry, Lord Bromley. It is just the promise of an affirmative endorsement in the future that we would like.'

'How old are you?'

'Nearly twenty.'

'Do you gamble?'

'Yes, sir.'

'And drink?'

'Copiously, my lord.'

A younger version of himself would have no doubt asked about the lad's bedding habits but the older one was tired of such debauchery.

'We will discuss it.'

'I am most grateful for such a consideration. I am also thrilled to be in your company, my lord, and wondered if you are by any chance going to the New Year's Eve party at the Jacksons tonight?'

'I wasn't thinking of it.'

'The wine is from France and the gambling tables are very rich.'

Nick did not feel like being alone again this evening. He felt restless and ornery, the anger in him over his visit to the river today growing. Perhaps if he went out it would help?

'Is your brother attending?'

'He said he might call in.'

'Wait until I change and I will join you. Help yourself to a drink.'

Once this would have been fun. Once he would have been the one to call for more wine and to set up games of chance that he had very little hope of winning. Once he would have had a woman on each arm and the promise of others all about him. Even now in the corner as far from the dance floor as he could manage he could see them observing him.

'Bromley? Is that you?' A particularly beautiful blonde came forward with a little entourage of more women of the same ilk. He felt like one of the sweetmeats he and Eleanor had probably fawned over in Fortnum and Masons all those years before.

Eleanor. He wished she was here with her wise eyes and laughter. He wanted her beside him more than he had ever wanted anything in his whole life.

'You must remember me, my lord. Diane Kennings. Now Mrs Diane Morningside.' If she could have added unfortunately without causing scandal he thought she might have. Nick had a slight recall of her visage through the drunken haze of sotted twenty-three-year-old eyes.

'We have heard such stories of your time away, Lord Bromley, and you have returned looking like a pirate.' The others giggled, but there was an undercurrent of anxiety.

The two men beside him whom he knew only vaguely looked on with interest, waiting for the start of a new scandal, he supposed. Once he would have enjoyed the challenge. Now he just wished fervently that young Christian Challenger might return forthwith, Frederick in tow.

'I don't think you can believe all you hear, Mrs Morningside. Mine is a fairly sedentary tale.'

'They say you got rich at the game of cards

and that you are every bit as reckless as you always were, my lord?'

The implication was clear as the woman flicked her fan this way and that.

'Age mellows one and a seat at the gaming tables has palled in its excitement. If I could give you any idea of my future intentions, I would probably have them as being a simple farmer.'

'At Bromworth Manor? Such a beautiful property, my lord. One of the finest in Essex, it is said.'

God, where the hell was Frederick? Nick looked around to see others glancing their way with as much interest on their faces as Diane Morningside seemed to have on hers.

How could he have possibly liked this, then? How could he not have seen the shallow amorality of such pointless conquests? He wished he did not remember all the many faces of his paramours, all the tears and pleading and the futile awful hope for so much more than he could give them.

Then Frederick was there and with a slight tip of his head Nick excused himself from the party and took him aside.

'I am leaving. Now.'

'I will come with you. You can drop me home.'

* * *

In the carriage five minutes later Nicholas leaned back against the leather cushion and began to laugh.

'Was it always like that?'

'As far as I can remember it was.'

'And we liked it?'

'Once we did.'

'Your brother Christian and his friends want to buy out my share of Vitium et Virtus. As far as I am concerned he can have it for free.'

'You've changed, Nick.'

'I know.'

'You seem happier.'

That wiped the smile off his face because he was happier and the person who was making him so was Eleanor Huntingdon.

'When you met Georgiana, how did you know she was the one that you wanted as a wife?'

'I could not stop thinking about her. She drove me so damn crazy I thought I would go mad.'

Hyde Park to one side was dark and cold as they passed it, small shadows in the undergrowth attesting to those who would sleep rough tonight. He was lucky with his friends and his house and his title. But he needed to protect himself and all those about him whom he loved.

'I'd like your help with something. Is there any chance of a meeting at Vitium et Virtus tomorrow at around noon? I'll ask Jacob and Oliver to be there as well.'

'It sounds serious.'

'It is, but it will be easier if we all put our heads together.'

'I'm glad you asked. Count me in.'

'I saw Nicholas earlier this evening.'

Georgiana Challenger looked up from her place on the thick rug at her husband's feet. The fire before them in their bedchamber was warm and inviting and Frederick had opened a bottle of fine wine to share.

'At the Jacksons' town house?'

'He asked me how I knew you were the one I wanted as a wife.'

At that she turned to kneel. 'He is in love?'

'Why would you say that?'

'It is a known fact that every young and worried husband-to-be asks exactly that question of his good friends.'

'How is it known? I have never heard of this truism.'

She placed her fingers against the line of his cheek, liking the way he smiled.

'Because it is a feminine knowledge. Who was he with there?'

'No one, although there were many female hearts a-fluttering.'

'I will ask Rose tomorrow. Perhaps she has some idea. Oh, I do hope I like her.'

Fred laughed. 'Only a woman would say something as ridiculous as that.'

'And only a man would not know exactly why Nicholas Bartlett was asking in the first place. What did you tell him in answer, anyway?'

'I said you drove me mad because I could not stop thinking about you.'

'Do I still do that? Drive you mad with desire?'

'Every single moment.'

'Frederick?'

'Yes.'

'I love you.'

Chapter Ten

Eleanor sat at her dressing table and peered at herself in the mirror. She looked older and more tired than she had ever been, lines of worry marring her forehead.

Lucy was back in London and she had spent the evening with her for she'd missed her daughter's laughter and hugs. She breathed out in worry for Jacob had asked Nicholas to their small family gathering tomorrow night and that definitely posed a problem.

Did Lucy look like him? Could the others possibly see the resemblance that she herself most certainly could? Would her daughter tell him how old she was in a passing conversation and if she did, was that something that he might consider and calculate? *'Five and nearly three-quarters.'* Children were never vague about their age.

No wonder she had lines on her forehead. Eleanor shut her eyes just to find a quiet that was missing inside every single thought she had.

It was Grandmama's fault. She had insisted on Nicholas Bartlett being there and for what reason Eleanor could hardly fathom. Something about promising his grandmother that she would watch over her grandson as the older woman was dying.

Eleanor wished her mother could have been standing behind her and running her soft hands across her hair, telling her that everything would work out fine and that worrying was just 'borrowing trouble'.

But it had not worked out fine at all when Mama had succumbed to the sickness of the lungs so quickly and had gone from them before anyone could even say goodbye.

Borrowing trouble? She inhaled slowly, one breath and then another. It was a trick she had perfected when Nicholas had disappeared and she had found out that she carried his child, when her whole world had shattered at her feet.

The calm came back and her glance fell to the small bracelet sitting beside her mother's silver brush.

She wished he had kept her token. She shook her head at that thought and wondered if in the six years of apartness she had learnt anything at all.

Nicholas had not kissed her. He had not remembered. Oh, granted he had held her with sensitivity after she had burst into tears, but he had let her go soon enough and gone back to the Bromley town house. With relief, she thought, if she'd read the look in his eyes properly.

She pulled her ring out from the neckline of the nightgown and stroked it.

'Please, please, God, let him love me.'

A knock at the door made her start and Rose appeared, her long blonde hair tied in a rough knot.

'I heard you talking and wondered who was in here.'

'Ghosts,' Eleanor replied. 'And deities.'

At that her sister-in-law came in and shut the door behind her to sit down on her bed.

'You have seemed busy lately? Jacob said you were helping Viscount Bromley retrieve his memory.'

'Well, it's not working.' She knew this sounded petulant, but it was good to speak to someone other than herself on the subject.

'What do you wish he would remember, Ellie?'

She turned at that to look at her sister-in-law and saw concern in the soft blue eyes.

'How much do you know of my past, Rose?'

'Very little, I think. I do understand that you have been lonely for all the time I have known you.'

God, was she meant to be near tears for ever today? She swallowed back hurt.

'I was never married. Not to the Highland Laird who died from a horse accident nor to the landowner in Edinburgh lost in a storm at sea nor, even, to any man in Scotland.' There, she had said it, just spat it out into the world for another to hear. Even Jacob and she had never been as honest on the subject. Rose, however, was perfectly pragmatic and blatantly unshocked.

'Well, it is nobody's business but your own, Eleanor, and I for one would never judge you.'

At that Eleanor smiled. 'I know.'

'And if this lack of a husband has anything to do with Nicholas Bartlett's disappearance then that is a conversation for the two of you only. But it is one you need to have.'

'How did you get so very wise?'

'A lifetime of adversity and hard work. Your brother has a lot to do with it, too. When you love someone beyond all else and they feel the same, every difficulty is lessened. Remember that.'

'Thank you, Rose.'

'You are most welcome, Eleanor. And I promise I will not say a word of any of this to Jacob until you say I can.'

Nick walked along the small alley behind the garden of Vitium et Virtus and imagined his younger self being ambushed here and dragged away. It was strange to have a knowledge of something, but no real memory. Jacob at his side slowed a little.

'Here.' He pointed to a spot beneath a spindly hedge. In summer it must have been thicker and greener. 'We found the blood right at this spot.'

'The ring we retrieved from over there beside that pile of stones. I had the impression you may have taken it off yourself to leave as a clue for us to find. If whoever did this to you had removed it, I think they would have recognised its value and kept the piece and it would never have surfaced again. Fred, Oliver and I searched the town for you the next day and when you hadn't turned up we went to Bromworth Manor. Your uncle said he hadn't seen you in a week.'

'I imagine he said that with a smile on his face.'

'If we knew then what we do now, we would have knocked the man's head off. The Night Watch got involved the following day, but no one had seen anything of you though one of the neighbours was sure he had heard a hackney cab careening in the area at around eleven.

'A month later we acknowledged the fact that you may be dead although in all the years since we never accepted it.' Jacob's frown was heavy. 'Perhaps we should have looked further afield, Nick, and searched for you in other places outside England.'

Nicholas shook his head. 'America is a big land and it is a long way from here. It would have taken a miracle to come across me there given I'd no idea of who I was anyway.'

'I can't help the feeling, Nick, that you would never have given up on us.'

'Lives are led, Jacob, and time passes. To rally against all the choices you could have made only leads to melancholy. You did what you could and in my book you did enough.

Today is the first day of the New Year. Let's look forward now instead of back.'

1819… Nicholas only wanted it to be a happy year. He'd wished for bigger things each new year when he was younger. More money. More parties. More women. In America he had never had the inclination for any dreams whatsoever. Now all he wanted was contentment.

And Eleanor. This thought had him breathing faster and he was glad Jacob, at his side, could not divine his thoughts.

The club appeared different in the light it was now in. Less new. More settled into its own skin. Familiar.

'We have had a good run here, haven't we? On the boat back from Boston I could see the place in my mind's eye looking exactly like this.'

'Rose was working here as a maid when I met her. Did you know that?'

He laughed. 'Every time one of you tells me something about your unusual women it surprises me.'

'Nothing is at it seems, Nicholas. You would do well to remember that.'

He did not have the time to dwell on such a cryptic remark because Oliver came down the steps to meet them and then Frederick arrived from the other direction. Both looked happy to see him, a smile on each of their faces, and Nick had the feeling that almost everything was right in his world. Breathing in and out deeply, he walked into the only true home he had ever had since losing his parents.

Inside they repaired to the private drawing room where he had first found them again, a high-stakes game of cards in play. Only six days ago? It seemed like a lot longer. When they were seated and the wine poured Nick brought the meeting to order.

'I have had word that the person who paid to have me murdered in the Americas was or is a member of this club.' He brought out the card the ringmaster had given him and laid it down. 'I was reliably informed that the gentleman who paid for the mark did so in gold and that he spoke like a lord.'

'You don't think it's any of us, do you?' Oliver asked this, shock in his eyes.

'Of course not. That's why I asked you here to help me catch him. If we could make a list of those who have a grudge against the club or even suffered a loss at one of the bigger card games, perhaps we might narrow the list down.'

Frederick answered that question fairly quickly, giving Nick the impression that membership was his domain. 'We have two hundred fully paid-up members now and a few who have left. But those who are accepted in usually end up staying.'

'Who have withdrawn?'

'Only a handful. Lance Grayson for financial reasons. Tony Shelkirk, because his wife insisted upon it. Frank Davis. Keith McNair. Nash Bowles, though he was kicked out.'

Nick's attention snapped in. Had he never told anyone of the man's perversion with the maid? 'Why?'

'Because he was a slimy perverted degenerate whom we could no longer stomach.'

'When did this happen?'

Frederick spoke then. 'About two weeks ago, after an altercation with Oliver.'

Nicholas cursed and was about to explain about encountering Bowles with the maid, when Fred carried on.

'But if he is on your list of suspects, Nick, there is a big difference between being a degenerate coward and an out-and-out killer. He's more of a nuisance, I think. Irritating and ineffective. He is also a cousin of Georgiana's stepmother.'

'All right. Who else?'

'David Wilshire. He issued you a death threat when Lady Hannah Goode kissed you in front of him, remember. He thought she had a *tendre* for him and then took umbrage when you won a large sum of money at cards from him a few hours later.'

'I met him a few days ago in Bullock's Museum. He is still unpleasant.'

'He was always a bit unbalanced at school, I thought. A boy one needed to be careful of.' Jacob pointed this out as he poured them all some more of the wine.

'What of your uncle's friend, Vince Matthews? He promised to see all of us in our graves for our poor behaviour and even wrote us a letter stating it.' Oliver frowned as he tried to recite exactly what had been in the missive. 'He said we were heathens who would be punished. He also warned us to watch our backs on dark and lonely nights.'

'But his was a more general warning to us all. It's specific threats we need, to Nick in particular.' Jacob stated this and the others agreed.

Half an hour later they had a dozen names. 'The club has a reputation for passion and temper. You have to expect these contretemps for it comes with the territory. It's like the army where there are always two sides to any argument and everyone wants to have their say.' When Frederick said this they all laughed. 'But it is good to be working together, to be sitting here and discussing problems and solving them again.'

Jacob lifted his glass to that and drank. 'Has there been any word of your guardian, Nicholas, since he left Bromworth Manor?'

'None. I understand he has gone to the Continent with what he could take of the family money. If he manages to stack away a reasonable amount and not spend it he might be able to stay away for ever. I won't be chasing him. As far as I am concerned he's dead and gone.'

'What of his son? He was a member here, if I recall, although I have not seen him lately.'

'I caught sight of him a month or so ago in town and he looked as angry as he usually does.' Oliver gave this reply.

'He would have the motivation to see you dead. Isn't he the next in line for the family fortune?'

'Unless I produce an heir, but it is rumoured that he has followed his father to the Continent.'

The realisation that more than one person wanted him dead made him feel vulnerable and sad. His life here had been fast lived and careless, so fast that he had numerous enemies waiting for their chance to strike.

Did Eleanor know of this animosity? Perhaps she had pulled back from him all those years ago because of it? The waste of living his life on the angry edge of a debauched underbelly made him see for the first time just how cunningly his uncle had encouraged him into such behaviour. His foolish recklessness had allowed Aaron Bartlett to manoeuvre himself into a stronger position financially in the taking of control of his inheritances. Hindsight was a fine thing, but he could barely believe he had not thought of this when he was younger.

'I don't believe Bartlett's son would be a threat anyway. He was always too much of a coward from the start.'

'Be thankful then for it. You could do with a few spineless adversaries, Nick.' The humour in Jacob's words was welcomed.

'Well, whoever it is will show their hand again and now that I have a better idea of who my opponent might be I will be ready for them.'

'We will all be ready for them.' Frederick laid down his hand and the others followed.

'In vitium et virtus.'

Nick only hoped it would be virtue that might win out.

Chapter Eleven

It was a small New Year's gathering, but Eleanor felt more nervous than she could ever remember being. Lucy was playing with her new china doll and her dolls' house, the front piece opened so that the rooms could be easily viewed as she sat at her chair and table to one side of the fire. On the other side on two large sofas her first cousin Frank Rogerson and his wife, Ilona, were in a lively conversation with Jacob.

Grandmama was asking Lucy about what was inside the rooms and Eleanor's daughter was giving her a running commentary on even the tiniest pieces of furniture.

'It's the smallest table in the world, Grammy, but it still has four legs and there are cups and plates that can sit on the top, see. If I pressed down hard I would squash it all to pieces like a giant.'

When did people lose that love of words, Eleanor thought as she watched her daughter, that uninhibited joy in all that was around them? She prayed that Nicholas might like Lucy. She also prayed that Lucy might like him.

The evening light was just fading as the Viscount arrived, shown into the front drawing room by the butler. As soon as he saw her he smiled, the dimple on his un-ruined cheek deeply etched in the light.

'Lady Eleanor.'

'Lord Bromley.'

They were formal here, polite and most correct, but she felt the thrill of his notice even as she stood and introduced her daughter.

'This is Lucy, my lord. She has just come back to London from Millbrook House.'

She could see the interest in his face. 'You look just like your mother.'

'That's 'cos I have the same colour hair, but mine's not so long.' Small hands brought her plait around to show him. 'But I like my red ribbon. I got it for Christmas from Mama. It has sparkles.'

When he nodded Eleanor could tell he had not been around children much, his face a picture of uncertainty and a kind of fright. So she helped him.

'Lucy was most fortunate this season and got a dolls' house and another dolly as a present. Would you like to show the house to Lord Bromley? I am sure he would love to see it.'

The thought hit her then just how much the Viscount's appearance contrasted so forcibly with their daughter, her child's soft perfectness balanced against his wounded hand in its sling and the terrible slash across his cheek. And yet in the way they held their heads and watched people there was a decided similarity. Her eyes were exactly his colour.

'You can play with the dolls if you want to. You can have the baby one because I don't like her clothes as much as the other new one,' Lucy chatted on as she found the swaddled china figure and held it out to him.

Without another option she saw Nicholas square his shoulders and walk forward to kneel to the side of the dolls' house.

Looking away, she caught her brother's glance upon her and flushed. Jacob was looking at her strangely and she could tell that he thought something was amiss.

She was not as small as he had thought she might be, this child of Eleanor's, but she was beautiful in the way of all little girls. He smiled at this because in truth he'd hardly had any contact with children in any part of his life.

Except Emily.

The name brought a cold rush of air into the warmth and his fingers shook as he held out his hand to receive a tiny china baby doll all wrapped in white cloth.

'You can put her to sleep if you like.' Up close he could see Lucy's eyes were not blue, but a warm golden brown.

'In here?' A miniature bed was in the room on the top-left storey and it seemed to be this she was pointing to.

'No, silly. That's a baby. She needs to go in the cradle, not the big girl's bed.'

Her hands found an even smaller piece of furniture, pink ribbons festooned in every corner and rockers beneath it.

'It even lifts up and down, see.'

And it did. The sides had been fashioned so that a lever could be pushed and the wood collapsed in on itself. With all the care in the world he placed the baby doll in its cradle and looked at Lucy for what to do next.

'Now we have to tuck her in. Here.'

A minuscule quilted pink blanket was then placed in his hands and he brought it over the doll, her fingers touching his as she finished the job for him.

She had dimples. Deep dimples on each cheek.

'Do you have a little girl, too?'

He shook his head.

'Mama only has me and I have her and Uncle Jacob and Aunty Rose and Grammy and Aunty Ilona and Uncle Frank and Vic.'

'Vic?'

'My dog. Vic is what we call him, but his long name is Victory. He is black and he always licks us, but Mama does not like that very much. He is this big.'

Little hands were held out as far as her arms could go, but Nick looked past this to Eleanor and saw the horror in her eyes. And the truth.

He cursed beneath his breath as the whole world dropped out of sight and he understood all that Eleanor Huntingdon had tried to hide from him.

Lucy was his. Theirs. Their daughter. Even without any memory he knew that she was. Her eyes. Her dimples. Her age. Her hair.

'How old are you, Lucy?'

'I am five years and three-quarters of months. My birthday is in May on the seventh and then I will be six. I know how to write my name and read, too. I can count to lots and lots. Do you want to hear how I can?'

As she began to count Nicholas's mind calculated the number of months between a week after August the fifteenth and May the seventh.

Nine months, give or take a few days. His vision lightened and his heart beat so fast in his temples he could not hear the spaces in between.

She had his eyes. That thought came through the shock. It was like looking at his own in the mirror, gold shards on the edge of brown. Her cheeks were his, too, high boned and broad. His gaze took in other parts of her greedily, desperately, trying to see everything at once and all that he had missed for so very long. She was perfect and flawless and splendid. He wanted to wrap his arms about her and never let her go.

Rose Huntingdon had bustled in and must have caught Lucy's recounting of her age because, suddenly, Rose was full of chatter. 'Oh, how lovely that you could come and have a supper with us, Lord Bromley, but you look a bit pale. I hope you are not catching a cold.'

Jacob began to rise with anger from his place near the fire and Rose peered at him sharply. 'Georgiana's cousin has been taken to bed for a month with an ailment of the chest and it is most important to consider one's actions carefully in the light of such information.'

Underneath the words Nick could hear a breathlessness and a warning and he wondered at Jacob's wife's strategies. Her fingers were tightly held before her, the reddened crescent of nails clearly visible on the soft white skin on each hand.

His daughter had risen at her words, her hand reaching out for Eleanor. Small hands still slightly rounded from babyhood. Every tiny detail of her was a joy to him.

'Dinner is served, so if you will follow me in. Grandmama, perhaps you could bring the Viscount. Ilona, you, of course, should accompany Frank. Lucy, as a special treat you can take Uncle Jacob's hand and sit with us for a little while before your nanny comes to fetch you. Eleanor, perhaps you and I could bring up the rear.'

Rose's voice was hard to hear through the rush of noise in his ears.

Eleanor felt cold with shock, though Rose's fingers against hers squeezed so tightly it brought her back with a desperate whisper.

'Get through the meal, Ellie, and then have your conversation. I will arrange it. But for now...'

Nodding, she took in a fearful breath. Frank and Ilona were lovely, but both were great gossips and she needed to hold on to her secrets until she could explain them properly. To Nicholas.

Rose had come into the room and heard Lucy, she was sure of it, for she had never seen her sister-in-law become quite so effusively shallow or overtly bossy. Even Grandmama was looking at her strangely. For such a deliverance Eleanor could only be eternally grateful.

Nicholas was seated as far away from her as Rose could manage, between Frank and his wife and opposite Grandmama, Lucy and she were at the other end of the table, Jacob and Rose between them. Everyone, save Lucy and the Rogersons, looked less than comfortable.

Eleanor could feel the Viscount's gaze upon her and Lucy, but didn't look up. She did not know how she might make it through a whole meal with the emotions that raced through her rendering her mouth dry and her pulse quickened. The grand clock in the corner showed only the hour of five forty-one.

She was glad for the wine that the footman poured and when Jacob finished his toast for the New Year she drank down a good portion of her glass. A temporary buttress, a provisional support. She waited as the footman topped it up again.

'Can I have some wine, too, Mama?' Her daughter's voice carried on the air and Nicholas Bartlett turned to listen to her answer.

'You may have some lemonade, sweetheart, but only a little as it is nearly bedtime.'

She was amazed her voice sounded so normal, so sensible, so very parental. The footman behind them half-filled her daughter's glass and then stood back.

'London suits you, Eleanor.' Ilona said this and her husband nodded his head. 'I said to

Frank this afternoon how very relaxed and content you look. I think you are losing years rather than gaining them.'

'It must be the Christmas season then, Ilona.' Her smile was tight and false. 'I always enjoy it.'

'It's a Huntingdon tradition to treasure family gatherings for the connections and discoveries they foster.' The darkness in Jacob's voice made Eleanor stiffen.

'We all of us enjoy it.' Rose added this quickly in a completely strained tone and the way she sat up so straight gave a clue as to how tense she really was.

'Jacob was informing us before your arrival this evening of your recent return from the Americas. Did you celebrate the Yule season abroad, Lord Bromley?'

'I lived mostly in the country, Mrs Rogerson. Christmas did not have a big presence there.'

'But you have been away a very long time?' The implication in Ilona's voice told Eleanor that her cousin's wife knew a lot more about his absence than she was letting on. Another problem. She was certain that the gossip of the Viscount's return had been as damaging and false as that of the talk of her own mysterious husband's death, embellished so much that even she had sometimes found the tales amusing.

'Too long, it seems.' Nicholas Bartlett's voice held a harshness she'd never heard from him before.

She felt a further rush of red come to her cheeks and caught the Viscount's glance at exactly that moment, the anger in his eyes clearly visible.

Anger. Of course he would be furious, but she had not even thought of that. She'd imagined questions or even joy. Such rage had her straightening in her seat and taking a breath. Two could play at this game and if he thought it had been easy for her all these years to be the sole parent of a child without a father then he had another think coming.

She would not cower.

So when Frank told a funny story about one of his childhood Christmases she made sure to laugh loudly and look as if she was enjoying the tale immensely. The wine helped, of course, and she was on her fourth glass before she saw her brother shake his head at the footman who came to refill it.

There was a bottle already left on the table of a fine red so she helped herself to the rest of that instead.

* * *

It was becoming easier, this charade, as time marched on and when Lucy's nanny came to retrieve her for bedtime at seven Eleanor made a show of kissing her daughter on the forehead and looking like the most congenial of parents.

'Say goodnight to everyone, darling.'

She had expected Lucy to simply bid the table adieu and was surprised to see her cross to each person and kiss them on the cheek. When she came to Nicholas she hesitated.

'Goodnight, Lucy.' He said the words quietly, the deepness of his voice filled with regret. Whether it was this or the wounds that he carried, but her daughter simply fell into his arms and kissed him twice.

'That one is for your hand to get better and that one is for your face. Mama always kisses my hurts better.'

'Thank you.'

Shame flooded her. Her small five-year-old daughter had acted with more grace than she had and as sorrow began to take over from false animation, all Eleanor felt was an endless tiredness.

She was careful to place her glass down on

the table before standing, the wobble in her voice presumably as noticeable as that in her gait. 'I think I should probably retire as well, as I have drunk far, far too much, so I wish you all a good evening.' She made a point not to look in Nicholas's direction at all.

Then she was free, walking out into the lobby and up the stairs, following her daughter to the nursery.

She could not talk to Nicholas tonight. Not like this. She needed to understand what she might say, needed to know just what she wanted from him as a father and as a man.

'He was nice, wasn't he, Mama? The man who came last. The one who played dolls with me.'

'He was, darling.'

Well, at least she had the answer to one of the questions she had posed herself earlier in the evening.

Her daughter liked Nicholas a lot.

Nick ate the cheese and figs and swallowed the last of his wine. When he looked at the clock it was just past nine and he knew he could not stay much longer, for more hours of smiling and pretence would simply do him in. His eyes went to the dolls' house Lucy had played with, the front of the edifice shut now and the dolls inside.

He loved her. He did. He loved his daughter so fiercely that it hurt his heart.

They had all lied to him. That thought was what had kept him rooted to the seat when Eleanor pleaded tiredness and excused herself. Jacob fidgeted in the way he always did when he was worried and Rose looked more and more desperate.

Only Grandmama kept smiling at him, her dark eyes watchful.

'Your grandmother would be pleased with how you have turned out, Lord Bromley, especially given your antics as a youth after the loss of your parents.'

He inwardly groaned. Was there nothing in this family that was off limits, no notice of that which was awkward or uncomfortable?

'You knew her well?' It was all he could think to say to try to divert her attention.

'Like a sister. We came out together and I was her bridesmaid when she married your grandfather. She was a strong woman just like Eleanor is with her own opinions and certainty.'

He suddenly understood where this was heading. My God, did the whole entire fam-

ily know what he had not? When he looked
across at Jacob he saw the apprehension on
his face was reflected in his wife's.

If Eleanor had not seemed more than a little
intoxicated he might have demanded to see
her right there and then, but Frank and Ilona
Rogerson were patently not in on the family
secret and he did not wish to make a fuss in
front of them.

So he did the next thing he could think of.
He finished off his wine and stood to take
his leave, insisting Jacob stay at the table
with his cousin and that he would let himself out.

A moment later he signalled to his driver
and waited till the Bromley conveyance came
to a halt beside him.

'The town house, please, Thackeray.'

It wasn't a long drive and as the horses
gained speed he leaned back and expelled
his breath. He would return in the morning and demand to see Eleanor Huntingdon,
that much he was certain of, for she and her
brother had lied to him about everything. The
implications of that rebounded in his head.
How many others knew of Lucy's parentage?
Were they ever going to tell him? Was there

some test he needed to pass before they considered him worthy?

A sudden noise caught his attention, the shout of strangers and the stoppage of the horses. Outside Nick saw two men running along the side of the carriage, their faces masked in cloth, weapons in their hands.

He was off his seat before he realised it, opening the door and jumping. He rolled up to a stand, not even feeling the heavy thump of the road in his anger, his arm shooting out and taking one of the hidden faces with his fist. When the man went down the second was already upon him and he felt the crunch of his nose as the man made a wild swing at him, the blood running thickly down the back of his throat.

Turning, he ripped the mask from his attacker's face. A snub-nosed stranger stared back at him, surprise about the only thing registering before he tore himself away and disappeared into the night, the iron bar he held clanking down on the street. When Nick looked around the other attacker was running, too, for a side alley a few yards up the road.

Panting with exertion, he came down on his haunches, trying to catch a breath, his left arm hurting like hell and his nose feeling painful and swollen. Then Thackeray was there, his voice unsteady.

'Shall I call somebody, sir.'

Nick stood. 'No. They have gone. Just take me home.'

Chapter Twelve

Eleanor had watched Nicholas Bartlett leave the Westmoor town house, his hat in hand and a heavy coat shrugged on in the winter chill of the night. She had been waiting for him to go ever since she had said goodnight to Lucy, not to hail or shout to, but just to observe.

He'd looked tired, his fingers threading through the hair at his temple, and she thought of the headaches he had told her of.

His hand was again cradled over his chest in the way he always held it if he thought no one was looking. Jacob had said the wound was substantial. A blade, he had intimated, that had cut the flesh to the bone.

The same blade that had glanced his cheek, perhaps? She wondered whether he would go home tonight as it was still early or whether he would head out again to enjoy the frivolity of the London night life.

If she knew exactly what it was she wanted from him, she would have run after him or waited downstairs to catch him as he left. But she did not even know that.

She had badly miscalculated the effects of being so secretive. Lucy did deserve to know him and Nicholas also needed to understand what had happened between them all those years ago so that he might make a decision based on facts.

The wine from dinner now sat in her stomach, souring her mood. The start of another year and here she was, in the place she had been for the past six of them, worrying again about her future and caught in a limbo.

Well, it would not do at all. She would go and see Nicholas Bartlett and explain her reasoning for such a subterfuge. Fear. Uncertainty. Years of making decisions about her and Lucy's life that had been entirely her domain.

Eleanor wondered whether the shock of understanding that he was indeed Lucy's father might have jogged other memories.

The heat of summer. The gauzy thin layers of cotton sheeting on his bed. The sound of

her heartbeat as he had leaned down to take
one nipple in his mouth.

Her breast rose even now at the memory
and she castigated herself for being so shallow, so very bent on the sensual. Last time
she had let her heart rule and not her head
and look what had happened.

She would go and see Viscount Bromley
in the morning before anyone here realised
she was gone and she would lay her cards on
the table with as much honesty as she might
muster. She hoped that it would be enough.

On arriving home Nick went straight to his
library to pour himself a straight whisky. The
shock of Lucy's parentage added to the attack
in the carriage had left him shaken and exhausted and he needed to understand just how
much of a threat these assailants could be to
Eleanor and his daughter, let alone to him.
This uncertainty needed to end. He needed
now to reclaim his own life, all of it, so that
the past and the present could lead to a future
that was decent and sustainable.

So he spent the rest of the evening sift-
ing through names on the list that he and the
others had drawn up in Vitium et Virtus. He

wrote down every single thing he remembered about the two attackers he had met tonight.

Both had carried weapons and had been dark haired. He'd scratched the first assailant on his cheek and the mark would undoubtedly last a while before it disappeared. If he could find this man before that happened...

But how?

Looking through the names, he kept returning to Bowles and Wilshire. Taking another page of paper, he drew a line down the centre and scrawled a list of any interaction he had ever had with either man. Bowles was the one who seemed to have more of a motive to hate him and yet Nick could not imagine why he would want to pay assailants over so many years to try to see him dead.

Unless...

What was it Eleanor had said of him? *There is something frightening about him.*

The incident at Vitium et Virtus had shown him that, the maid Bowles had hurt with his small sharp knife shaking in fear and pain. What might have happened if he had not chanced upon the pair when he did? Could Nash Bowles have taken things even further? If he had been hanging around the club, perhaps the others might have noticed other situations that were similar?

Nick's head was starting to ache with all the possibilities and he leaned back against the soft leather and watched the fire.

Flame had always calmed him. He'd spent a month in a cold, hard-floored jail outside New York after being accused of cheating in a card game by a man who was later found dead. It was winter and he had nearly frozen to death by the time they let him out, the charges dropped altogether when witnesses to the murder and the actual culprit had come forward.

After that he had gone into the wilderness and built a fire at his campsite every night right through to the springtime.

Taking a sip of his whisky, he felt the warmth of it slide downwards as the clock on the mantel chimed the hour of three.

Another thought struck him. At Bullock's Museum the other day when he had met David Wilshire, the man had informed him that Nash Bowles had not forgiven him, a fact alluding to strong feelings especially after six years of absence.

Why would that be? Surely Bowles would have realised his actions at Vitium et Virtus were despicable at the least and moved on?

Outside the moon passed behind a cloud and the room darkened. Nicholas seldom sat up at night with a light on, save for that of the fire. Years of hiding had taught him the shadows were safer places in which to dwell and to be hidden.

He wished Eleanor were here to talk to for only with her did his sadness lift and disperse and he yearned to know more of the little daughter that they had made together.

Lucy. He wondered if she had been given a middle name.

A pile of notebooks he had taken from Vitium et Virtus sat on the table beside him, tomes that described some of the day-to-day happenings at the club that had been kept as a reference by Jacob, Frederick and Oliver ever since he had left. He flipped over the first page of the top book and smiled as he slanted it to firelight. Jacob presumably had drawn a couple in full mask at a ball. The notes below described the night in detail—those who had attended and those who had won or lost at the card tables.

The rest of the book was in the same vein, he saw, as he kept on turning the pages, though towards the end a passage from two weeks ago caught his whole attention.

'Nash Bowles has been harassing a number of the patrons with his particular kind of unsuitable lust and when confronted by Oliver he asked if we believed Nick to be dead. Oliver's hand was injured by Bowles's blade and he told him to forget Nicholas for it was no business of his anyway.'

Nicholas could almost hear Oliver giving the warning in his direct manner. But why would Bowles even ask such a question?

He could well have been killed a number of times in the Americas, but it was too far-fetched to imagine Nash Bowles paying for someone to stalk him thousands of miles from home.

Yet Nicholas felt as though he was missing things. It was late and he was tired and the stamina he might have had in his early twenties was wilted at almost thirty. His searing headache probably did not help, nor the throbbing pain in his left hand and fingers. Stretching out, he grimaced as a shot of white heat buried into the bone at his wrist without warning and did not relent.

He'd been hurt so very often. The gunshot at his thigh. The more recent knife wound to his face and hand and the strips of scarring on his back from the jail in Boston. But this time everything was different for he did not want to be shunted on to another location to find safety. This was where he must stand up and meet the one that wished him harm, head on and with determination. He had the help of his friends and the resources of the Bromley fortune. He had the motivation and he also had the fury.

His eyes went across the darkened stains of blood on the breast of his jacket and the dried brownness of it on his fingers. He should wash, he knew, but somehow such stains gave him strength and courage. A badge of resolve and tenacity, his vehemence harnessed by something more than just himself now. He had a daughter to protect and he had Eleanor. It was time to bring the fight out into the open and end it once and for all.

Leaning back in fatigue, he gave consideration to the fact that it was now the second day of the new year.

A sign. A direction. He closed his eyes and dozed.

The doorbell rang before the hour of ten in the morning, waking Nick with a start for he wondered just who on earth would come to see him this early.

'Lady Eleanor, my lord.'

She was there in his library even as his man stopped speaking, pushing in behind him and coming into the room.

'Thank you, Browne. That will be all.' He tried to keep the surprise at seeing her from his eyes, but he was disorientated and cold and his arm hurt like hell. Last night's soiled clothes were still upon him although he hoped he had washed all the blood off his face.

'You have not slept?'

Her words were laced in question.

'Did you?' He made a point of looking across at the time.

'No. I lay awake all night and wondered what I should do.'

'Honesty,' he drawled, 'may have come a little late for me, Eleanor.' Her eyes were ringed in the same darkness he knew his own would be.

'There is no good time to tell a man you have not seen in six years, and who cannot remember you at all, that he is now the father of your child.'

He laughed at that because the words were so quintessentially Eleanor.

'Were you going to enlighten me if I had

failed to guess the truth or made no progress in regaining my memory?'

When she lifted her left hand to her temple in a gesture of complete worry he saw she wore her small braided bracelet with the colourful beads around her thin wrist and the fight went out of him just like that.

'I want to know you, Eleanor. I want to remember you.'

The blue in her eyes blazed.

'Well, I am running out of days to try and help your recall. After tonight—the sixth day we spent together—I do not know what happened next, for it was the last time I saw you.'

'What happened the last time I saw you, Eleanor?'

'You asked me for dinner at your town house.'

'Here? Alone? Just us?'

She stood stock still and quiet against the backdrop of his dimly lit library. Her lips were pursed and her hair was jammed under another of her horrible hats. There was a pin in the felt, enamelled in the colour of the butterfly wing he had seen in Bullock's Museum, the one that had exactly matched the blue of her eyes.

'I was young and foolish and my mother

had just died and I was lost in thrall to you, lost in the hope of something I had no knowledge of. That is why I came here, then.'

A tear ran down her cheek, the splash of it darkening the lighter collar of her cloak, but she made no attempt at wiping it away, merely watching him through the awful horror of truth. She looked beaten and some hard-formed part of him broke with her distress as he stood to move forward.

'It was not your fault, Eleanor. It was all mine. I was older than you and arrogant, and what I desired I took. I am sure that that was how it was and it should not have been so.'

But she spoke then with the utter conviction of the damned.

'No. When you kissed me that first time at Lackington's I wanted it all, more, everything that you knew. Two days later I peeled away my bodice even as you tried to stop me in your bedchamber and by then it was far too late for the both of us. I had not worn undergarments, you see.'

'Hell.' He did see. The most beautiful woman in all the world offering her naked body to him without conditions or reservation. Even a saint would have had a hard job denying such a gift and he had never been one.

Had he said he loved her? Had he at least given her that to hold on to as a troth in the many years of his absence? He could not ask because a negative answer would lessen everything. He needed to make things right. He needed to court her in the way the sister of a duke would expect to be. He needed to reinstate her absolute value.

'Come to dinner tonight, Eleanor. Here. With me.'

For a moment he thought she might not answer him at all, but then she did.

'Why?'

'I want for you to understand that it was not all a lie, our past. That the truth was there, too.'

'What time should I come?'

'Eight o'clock.'

He breathed out because the relief was so great.

'I am not sure of who I was six years ago, but I was not the man I should have been and I am sorry for it.'

She smiled at that. 'Perhaps I was different, too. Sillier. More unwise.'

He shook his head. 'I cannot even imagine you as that, Eleanor.'

'Immature then. Impossibly romantic.'

* * *

She could sense his closeness and his urgency and the stretched want of him and she knew a madness that had been there before in her. Uncloaked again. Let free.

Touch me and we shall both burn down to ashes.

She wanted to warn him as she had not, then. She wanted to shout such concern out loud here in the quiet of his library in the dulled light of a grey morning.

But she didn't because every single part of her tingled with the need to feel him against her. She had never met another like him. Then and now. But especially now with his strength and his distance and a hardness that had risen from all that was softer.

'May I kiss you, Eleanor?'

'Yes.' The word tangled in her throat even as she whispered it when he came closer. An elemental knowledge. The shivers chased each other across her skin and pulled up her spine.

Yet she didn't go lightly into his embrace, for she was no young girl any more, the tears from before dried salt upon her cheeks. No, she went with hesitation across the few footfalls and came up against warmth; the quiet silence between them full of sound, breath and heartbeat.

Her defences were breached and broken, every reason she knew she should not be here drowned by the arguments that she should. Her arms came around him and she closed her eyes against the moment, only feeling. With trepidation she took in a breath and waited.

One finger touched the line of her cheek, feather-light. 'You are so very beautiful, Eleanor. More beautiful than any woman I have ever known and you are brave, too, which I thank you for.' She looked at him then, directly, as his hand travelled upwards tracing the tip-tilt of her nose and the shape of one eye and then threaded through her hair at the temple, all the time the pressure building.

His mouth came across her own, sealing intimacy, the heat of his flesh and the push of his tongue. He was greedy in what he took, shaking away her small offering and coming in further. His good hand cradled her head so that the kiss could deepen and he could know every part of her, her whole body bound up in his own. Wanting.

And then the dam broke, the gentleness replaced by only need and the hot savage touch of his lips against hers. She pushed against the tautness in her own desperation.

Do not make this gentle, Nicholas. Do not kiss me as if I might break. Please.

As though he understood he suddenly brought his mouth in from a different angle and took her without restraint, a demanding kiss that promised everything. Sensation scorched through her body, in her stomach and between her legs and in the tight pull of her nipples against the lawn of her petticoat.

This is what she had dreamed of for all those years. Exactly this. And her release came with barely a warning, the edges of lust opening and beaching across the shattered pieces of her soul.

Only him. Only her.

She clung to him as if he was the last salvation between her and eternity.

He could feel her release, strong and then stronger, the clutching waves of passion making her throw back her head and groan. No longer a duke's sister. No longer the careful Eleanor Huntingdon who seldom showed her colours either. Here with him she was somebody else. Dangerous. Vulnerable. Recklessly unsafe. The sting of her fingernails carved small troughs down the side of his neck.

He knew now that he could take her, that he could simply lift her up and carry her to his bed. The old Nicholas would have done exactly that and without compunction, but something inside him had changed and instead he drew her close to his body and held her, the hard ache at his groin pressed into her cloak.

Not like this, he thought. Not again.

But his heart thumped with the shock of her and the want, for all the shadows of who he had been were pushed into a corner by her light.

With Eleanor he could live again. With her he could be healed of bitterness and of loss. The smell of violets made him smile into her hair, soft curls of brown and gold tumbling under his chin.

She was so fragile in her honesty that it frightened him.

Take it slow, he thought. Let her get used to you and know you. Let her understand that this was a mutual want and that they had all the time in the world to understand it.

'I am sorry.' Her words, hot against the skin at his throat.

'For allowing me to kiss you?'

Her head shook. 'For being so…wanton.'

He laughed at that and his grip strengthened. 'You think I might want a milk-sop girl who hardly moves or breathes, but simply stands there as I kiss her?'

'I do not know.'

And she didn't. She had made love to him for one night all that time ago and then been thrown into the lonely winter of widowhood for six long years until tonight. Until now.

'You are perfect, Eleanor. In every way possible.'

She stilled and pulled back, looking up at him as if he was giving her an untruth.

'Tonight I will show you exactly how I mean it.'

'The dinner?'

'And more if you will allow me. Much more if you stay with me.'

The beat of his heart was heavy as he offered her himself.

He would remember this moment, this second scrawled into faulty memory. In the reds of the fire and the warmth of her skin. In the grey of the morning and the silence in the room, save for breath between them, ragged in need.

He'd been trapped in time for so long and

to suddenly be released to feel again, to walk and love and laugh, was overwhelming. The joy of her filled him, overflowing, her fierceness and her beauty, the grace of rediscovery, the benediction of touch. He let her go when she pulled away because he wanted to do nothing to frighten her.

'I will see you tonight, Nicholas.'

It was the first time she had called him by his Christian name and he was heartened by the fact. Then she readjusted her hat and was gone.

Eleanor lay down upon her bed when she got home and buried her head in a pillow.

My God, had that just happened? Had she truly been so very shameless? He had known what had transpired inside her for he had said as much and yet he'd stood there, composed and collected, watching on as she simply went to pieces.

Even now the echoes of what she had felt gripped her insides, sliding their treachery into the heated folds of her skin.

In penance or in vindication, she knew not which.

All she did know was that for years she had felt nothing, wanted no one, the emptiness and void of her life without Nicholas welcoming oblivion.

It was for Lucy that she had kept going, kept breathing, kept imagining that he would come back, alive and whole and loving.

Well, here he was, offering her his bed and his touch and his body. Not the love words yet, she thought with a frown, and remembered how distant he had been last time after she had allowed him everything.

She rolled over and looked up at the ceiling. Tonight she would go to his bed and know him again. Her hand came over her mouth, in both worry and in delight. But she would not falter, not now, when the world was being offered back to her, without condition.

She was twenty-four years old, soon to be twenty-five, and she had slept with only one man for one night in all her life. Him.

She felt breathless and light headed and slightly sick.

She had been thinner then, more girlish, but the long lines of eighteen had formed into softer curves at twenty-four. Would he like the change? Would he notice the small white marks of motherhood that had appeared across her stomach, muted, she knew, but nevertheless there?

She sat up, her hands held tight across her middle as the worry inside her grew. What if he did not love her in the same way? What if she got pregnant again and he left, this time for greener pastures and more beautiful women?

But the night was like a treasure offered, a place to start again, a way of reconnection that was as absolute as the desperation she felt for him. She would not give the chance of it up for anything.

Crossing to the mirror at her dressing table, she sat at the stool there. The woman who looked back at her was a stranger, for excitement pooled in her eyes and the streak of animation on her face made her look so completely different. Almost beautiful. When she moved, her smile ran into the rainbow edges of the glass and she saw herself a dozen times or more, stretching back into the distance.

Multiplied. Proliferate. That was how Nicholas Bartlett had made her feel right from the very first second of meeting him.

A small sound at the doorway alerted her to the presence of another and she turned to see her daughter there, three dolls all tucked in a basket that she held.

Opening her arms, she waited until Lucy

was within them and turned to the mirror again, her child on her lap.

'What do you see, Lucy?'

'Me and my mama. You are smiling a lot, but your hair looks messy.'

'I see my beautiful daughter and her three small friends.'

'I see rainbows there—' little fingers touched the bevelled edges '—and here I see your eyes. They are bright blue and mine are brown. Where does eye colour come from?'

'From your mama and your papa.'

'But mine is gone.'

'No.' Eleanor squeezed tight and looked at Lucy through the glass. 'No, he is not gone for good, my darling, and one day soon you shall meet him and he will love you.'

'All the way to heaven and back?'

'That's a very long way, but, yes, all that way and more.'

Chapter Thirteen

An hour later Eleanor rummaged in her wardrobe to try to find a newer version of the same dress she had worn before at the Bromley town house. A dark primrose gown, with embroidery around the bodice and the bottom of the sleeves.

The décolletage was low, but she heightened it with a swathe of ivory Brussels lace that had been her mother's. Today she needed courage and conviction. After this morning it was time to face the ghosts of the past whether Nicholas remembered what had happened or not.

He had been ill shaven when she had visited him and the jacket he'd worn had been covered with bloodstains. Another contretemps, she thought. A further recklessness.

Was his life going to be blighted by such

violence for ever? Today he had not looked angry, only sad. That had thrown her more than the fury.

It was not his fault he had been shanghaied into a journey to the Americas and yet...

It was not her fault she had fallen in love with him so quickly and allowed him everything and yet...

They were both to blame for what had happened six years ago. There was only the desires of the present in all that they had done, the thrill of the flesh and the forbidden.

She had just lost her mother then and Nicholas's uncle was becoming more and more impossible. Each to the other was a way out, a way to forget.

But now...

She liked him more as a man.

Stay here with me.

She swallowed hard and stood to look out the window into the winter. She knew what she wanted. Last time they had laid together it had been in the summer warmth. Now it was cold, but if they could find a path back to each other the spring came next and then new life. The smaller niggle of uncertainty also crept back again. He had never said that he loved her.

There was a knock on the door and Jacob's head appeared.

'Can I come in?'

'Of course.' She knew her brother would want to have a conversation after the events of last evening.

'Nick thinks Lucy is his, Ellie. I can see it in his eyes.' Jacob did not beat about the bush and, given his lack of addressing her pregnancy this directly before, she was shocked because it was a statement more than a question. After her conversation with Rose she knew she owed him at least the truth.

'He wants to talk to me tonight. At Bromley House.'

'Is it true, Eleanor? Is he the father?'

'Yes. We slept together once the night before he disappeared.'

'Why didn't you tell me?'

'Because you were too sad. Because you had just lost him and I knew that you would not be able to bear hearing his name everywhere in our house and in the tragedy of what had happened to me.'

'Nicholas will marry you. I know he will. It is his responsibility and his duty.'

She smiled. Another honourable man. Her brother.

'It is not quite as easy as that, Jacob. He has changed and so have I. We are different people from those that we were.'

'You are parents of a little girl who needs a mother and a father.'

'And you think I do not understand that? You think I don't wonder about this every single moment?' Her ire had built and Jacob raised his hands.

'I am of the belief that every problem well discussed can be solved.'

The truth of that advice comforted her, made her calmer.

'Which is the reason I am going there to see him tonight.'

With that he moved forward to kiss her on the cheek. 'Then the carriage will be at your disposal and Rose will watch over Lucy. I will leave it to you to give the driver his instructions. Whatever you choose those instructions to be, they will be no one's business save your own. If you are not home tonight, then I will see you on the morrow. I have every faith that you can make this right.' Then he was gone.

Nicholas moved a pile of books from one desk to the next in his upstairs sitting room.

He had a roaring fire and good wine. Dinner would be served in an hour on the small table here. For the only time in his life he had asked the cook if he could peruse the menu.

He was nervous. He admitted this to himself as he paced the room. If this went badly...

'No.' He shook his head and caught sight of his reflection in the mirror above the fireplace. The scar blazed red on his cheek and his nose was swollen from the carriage incident last night.

A noise from further afield told him Eleanor had arrived. He could hear her voice through the silence and then footsteps coming up the staircase. Tonight he had given all the servants, save for a few, the night off.

'Lady Eleanor Huntingdon, my lord.' Browne was the soul of discretion and formality.

She stood very still in her cloak, a dark woollen sheath that enveloped her completely. She did not speak at all as the door closed, but simply stayed there looking at him.

'Thank you for coming.'

She nodded at that, both hands tightly clasping the brocaded edges of her apparel.

'It is warm in here,' he said. 'Perhaps I could take your cloak?'

Her eyes went to the fire and she tugged

at the fastening at her neck. Tonight she was in yellow, a dark yellow that picked up the lighter strands in her hair and the curve of her figure. The frothy cream lace at her throat suited her as did the way she had done her hair. It was not fussy. She had pulled the mass of it into a loose pile at the back of her head, the curls that had escaped making her look younger. More uncertain. Beautiful.

The kiss from this morning still simmered in the air around them and he made sure he did not touch her, not yet, not until they had spoken of their daughter for there was so very much he wanted to know.

'We need to talk, Eleanor. About Lucy.' When she nodded he waited.

'I am sorry for the way you found out about her existence. It was unacceptable.' The crisp sound of the word rolled from her tongue in a way that only she could say it.

Unacceptable. To her?

The frown line between her eyes was deep, her lips pursed in on each other in consternation.

'In my defence I might say that your coming back was indeed a surprise and that I was caught in uncertainty.'

'Does Lucy know that I am her father?'

'No.' He saw her swallow back emotion and saw her flinch, too, when he used her name.

Turning away, he poured them each a drink, handing a glass to her with care.

He wished he had not asked the question so baldly. He wished he could take it back and say it differently. She had been here only a few moments and already the barriers between them were rising.

'I bought her something today.' Crossing the room, he took out a small burgundy box and then placed it in Eleanor's outstretched palm.

'For Christmas?'

'No. For ever.'

At that she half-smiled and, opening the lid, brought out the small gold locket in the shape of a heart that he had purchased from the jewellers Rundell, Bridge & Rundell in the early afternoon.

'Perhaps it is not something a small girl might want...' He stopped.

'She will love it.'

Her hand reached out to touch his arm in reassurance and he felt the heat of it physically, the same punch of lust he was becoming used to in her company.

Go slow, his mind warned. Do not frighten

her. He held his want in such check that he trembled with the effort and was glad when the small cuckoo clock chose that moment to beat out the hour, breaking the pressure into fragments that were less sharp and more manageable.

'It's never worked properly.' His words, falling into the silence. 'My grandmother bought it for me years ago.'

'Ten minutes late is not too late, I should imagine.'

He swallowed away thickness. She often phrased her words like no one else did.

An image of the piano came, her fingers across his and tears in her eyes. And then left. The suddenness of it was shocking.

Bits. Pieces. Nothing.

Putting down his glass, he ran one hand through his hair, trying to soothe the ache that was building in his temples, trying to right the imbalance.

'It was here we slept together?' He could hear the truth of it in his own question.

'Only once.' Her answer.

And once had been enough. Lucy. Eleanor's enforced widowhood and years away from the *ton*. She had been eighteen and alone, the kind and obedient only daughter of a duke when he had come into her life. One night had demanded a large payment.

'Was anyone with you for the birth?'

'Grandmama. Lucy was born at Millbrook.'

'I should have been beside you.'

'The midwife was a great believer in the idea of men being nowhere near a birthing room.'

'Was Jacob at the manor?'

'Yes.'

A stab of jealousy pierced his equanimity.

'My papa was there, too, and he thought Lucy a miracle. Mama had died the year before and his sadness was lessened by her coming. A new life, I suppose, and new hope for the future, despite the circumstances.'

'Was she a little baby?'

Eleanor nodded. 'Small and perfect. She had blonde hair and then it turned darker on the ends so that she looked like a porcupine with its quills sticking out.'

He drank up such words like a man who had been lost in the desert for days without water, imagining.

'She walked when she was ten months. She simply stood up and took six steps. Two weeks later she was almost running.'

'Clever girl.'

'Her first word was "dog". Then she said "Mama" and she has never stopped talking since. She is learning the piano. She loves to dance. She puts on shows for us and we all buy little tickets to watch. Vic is one of her main players.'

Nervousness always made Eleanor talk and he smiled, liking every single thing he learned.

The silence re-gathered.

'Does she have a middle name?'

'Christine. After my mother.'

Please, God, do not let me cry.

Eleanor could see his eagerness and his loss, the poignancy of all those missed years written in every line of his face.

The golden heart was warm in her hand. When she flipped the necklace over she saw the Bromley family crest had been engraved on the back of it. Another effort that told her of his hopes.

His hair was wet, the curls falling with loose dampness upon the white of his collar and the jacket he wore was tight enough to define the muscle beneath the fabric.

How easy it would be to simply move forward and fall into his arms. With hope. But she had to know him first, had to understand what it was he wanted of them.

Was Lucy the only thing that held them together now? Just the promise of her? Eleanor drank the wine and liked the feeling of how it bolstered her courage. Ever since he had come back she had drunk much more than she had before.

Another difference. She struggled for a further topic, but he spoke before she could.

'How did we meet, Eleanor? I remember you only as the much younger sister of Jacob whom I seldom saw?'

'I had gone to the Vauxhall Pleasure Gardens with my grandmother and her friends to see the fireworks and you were watching me. When Grandmama was busy, we spoke.'

'Just spoke?'

'You touched me.'

And I thought I had been burned by flame.

'How?' He had moved closer now.

'You took my hand and kissed the inside of my palm. The darkness allowed it. I knew you, of course, but at first you did not know me. The orchestra was playing Handel and when it was supper I escaped to eat it with you. Cold meats and cheese and puddings. You held a silver pass for the season and pots of beautiful red and blue flowers hung from every tree above our heads. The air smelt of fireworks.'

'You remember details.'

Every single one of them, she felt like saying, but didn't.

He wanted to remember so badly.

'Did I kiss you?' His finger reached out to touch her lips softly.

'Not properly.' She blushed bright red as she said this and he thought such reticence did not sound like him. When he desired something he had usually taken it without worrying about consequences. Then.

'You kissed my hand and my wrist. Just there. Then Grandmama came to find me and you disappeared.'

Interrupted as he would not be tonight.

'Can I try again? Now?'

Staying just where she was, she lifted her hand and he turned it over, his thumb stroking the patterns there carefully.

He could feel her draw in a shaky breath and was glad when her eyes came up to meet his, the blue in them as startling as he always found it.

'And then you say I kissed it?'

She nodded, fear overwritten by something else entirely.

'Like this?'

She tasted of lemon and salt and woman. His tongue drew along the same pathway his thumb had just left and he could smell the violets imbued in her skin.

The yellow gown was long sleeved so he pushed away the fabric to measure the pulse there with his lips. Fast and shallow. His own was probably much the same.

The first salvo was fired and, releasing her hand, he took his wine from the table nearby and held it out to her.

'To beauty and to memory, Eleanor. And to Lucy, our daughter.'

She drank to that, her lips leaving a mark on the glass that he then covered with his own.

He was a thousand times more dangerous than the man she used to know, the light playfulness gone and in its place a scorching sensual certainty. He was also promising her nothing save for this one night.

Her worry increased. What if his memory was suddenly jogged back and he recalled how he had pulled away last time? A lover who thought she had not quite been enough? A man who had sampled all that she'd offered and decided it wasn't for him?

A hundred thoughts whirled around in her mind, a vulnerability that had been so complete six years ago she had barely survived and one that she was only just now beginning to recover from. Could she chance it all again or should she leave?

Her heart sank at such a thought.

Tonight he had allowed her the space to come to terms with what he wanted, but he would not be denied. She knew that to the very core of her soul.

The wine was an interlude to be enjoyed, but that was all. The stories that she had heard of him through the gossip mills of the *ton* had been running around for years, but the living and breathing reality was so much more overwhelming.

She ought to call a halt to what he was proposing, cry enough and leave before she lost any will to say no. On his terms. Again.

'I think perhaps I should eat. The wine is strong.' She sounded like her grandmother, the rigid tones of sense discordant after the softer ones of lust.

His smile sent her heart into further spasm.

Sensing her fear, he rang the bell on the small table beside him and instructed the man who came to serve the dinner immediately.

'Can I show you to your seat?'

When his hand came up under her arm she felt the spark of connection like a shock.

It was a small table and they sat close. As the creamy chicken soup was served she saw the footman did not tarry, but rather closed the door behind himself and left them alone. When Nicholas locked it she was glad. Without interruption she could speak to him properly.

'It was not my intention to deceive you about Lucy for I thought you were dead.'

'To an extent I was. Deception is an emotion I have had lots of practice in, for when you do not know who you are you can be anything at all and make others believe it, too.'

She smiled at that because she understood the concept entirely. 'And who were you? Then?'

'A traveller. A businessman. A tramp. A card player. An outsider. It depended on the time of year and the places I was in. Summer usually found me in the back country far away from anyone. In winter I had to return to civilisation and shelter.'

'A hard life for a lord?'

'At first it seemed worse because, I suppose, I was softer.'

She could imagine him as a twenty-three-year-old without memory thrown into the chaos of a new country, without money, without a name.

'Who were you there? How did you call yourself?'

The brown of his eyes was full of harsh memory.

'A variety of different names all cobbled together by expediency. I was Peter Kingston when the man who did this found me in the town of Richmond tending a bar.' His good hand gestured to his bad one and at his face.

'It had been a while since I had moved so I was feeling safer and it was a shock when he tried to kill me as I was gathering wood for the fire from a shed by the river.'

'Did you know him?'

'No. But I did not know the others, either.'

This truth nearly broke her heart because in those few words she could imagine exactly just what his life there had been like.

As if he thought he had said too much he raised his wine glass, struggling for a lost ease.

'But tonight I am in the company of beauty,

grace and honesty, so here's to the future, Eleanor. And here's to faith.'

'Faith?'

'In that future. Faith to decide how we go on from now.'

'Where do you want us to go?' The words came unbidden, tumbling out over the top of her more normal caution.

'I'd like to do away with your Scottish husband for a start.'

She could see naked desire scrawled across his face and the thick soup of chicken, veal and almonds became dry in her mouth. She was also far too hot. With care she removed her lace fichu, squaring her shoulders so that the bodice was not quite as revealing as it might have otherwise been.

'The story of my marriage was Jacob's idea. A way to protect me from the censure of society.'

'And I thank him for it.'

'But I promise that I never gave Lucy the same lie.'

He looked up at that, the gold chips on the edge of his irises caught in the firelight. 'What did you tell her?'

'That her father loved her. That one day he would be back because I…'

She stopped.

Loved him.

How easy it would be to simply move forward and fall into his arms.

The muscle along the side of his jaw moved, the scar on his cheek standing out further because of it. 'I am grateful, Eleanor.'

And just like that she was back again, back six years sitting opposite him in front of the fireplace in his room.

I am grateful, Eleanor.

His words then, when they had dressed finally and he had got ready to return her home. She had sensed his distance then, but it was different now. Could the wasteland of the years lost finally end in salvation?

She laid her hand gently down across his damaged hand, feeling the ridge of bandages end under the fabric of his sleeve.

'Once, I hoped that you loved me.'

There, it was said and she did not wish to take it back. If she was to trust him, she needed to have faith.

His other hand came down over hers, warm and solid.

'Hoped?'

'You did not say it, but…'

He swore softly, their fingers intertwined.

'Sometimes I barely even like the man that I was and I should not have—'

She didn't let him finish.

'Being together was a mutual decision and if you didn't say the words then—'

He placed his finger on her lips to stop her from admitting more.

She was frightened. He saw that her whole body shook with it. She had given her eighteen-year-old self to him, then he had disappeared and ever since…?

He was still dangerous to her, the attack from the early hours of yesterday morning leaving him agitated and on edge. He should make her go home to her brother and to safety, but in her words there were things he could no longer ignore. Nicholas had to tread carefully for it seemed that last time he had not.

'Our daughter looks like you, but her eyes are mine.'

He could see her listening. Lucy was the centre of her world and it was a way in.

'She has dimples, too.'

That brought a nod.

'Could I meet her as her father, Eleanor? I would very much like to do that.'

He was gentle with his request. He took nothing for granted with his rights to see his daughter. It was her decision alone to allow it…or not.

'Yes,' she whispered, her eyes meeting his exactly and the fright there eased.

The soup was finished now and he knew he should open the door and ask for the next course to be brought in, but he couldn't move.

One finger ran across the length of her thumb and across to the forefinger. She had freckles on the bridge of her nose and he looked at the smattering with a smile.

'How could I forget this, Eleanor? How could I forget you?'

His whole mind struggled for a glimpse of her from back then, at Gunter's or Lackington's or here, but there was nothing save the ache of the trying for recall in his temples.

'Last time we were here it was summer and the candles were warm because there were so many. After the dinner you loosened my hair…'

He stood at that and drew her up with him, their bodies almost touching as his hands rose to the pins she had tied it back with and he carefully drew them away. The brown curls fell in a curtain down to her waist, unravelling into silk.

Unravelling like his caution and his ever-present distance.

The floor tilted as he pulled her to him and took her mouth, not with softness but with a hard and desperate need, his hands at her nape as he slanted the kiss.

'Eleanor.' Her name was groaned in a broken whisper as he brought her closer.

He kissed her completely differently now. Before he'd left England he had been more careful and softer, but now he held a scorching sensuality that made her head spin.

She clung to his heat and took the offered breath as he seized what he wanted, quick and desperate. She heard the guttural sounds she made, but could not stop them, her breath slowed into only desire, her body melting into need.

'Nicholas?' Breathed out as his tongue came around the fullness of her lips, the feel of it shocking.

Her own mouth opened and she let him in to taste and to savour. There was no reason in their kisses now, logic lost beneath feeling until he turned her abruptly and his teeth fastened on the skin of her throat. She keened into the silence and pressed into him with demand.

Every touch he gave her left her more naked in spirit than the one before. She was stripped down into an intensity that held no fight whatsoever.

He could do as he wanted with her and he knew it. She could see it in the velvet brownness of his eyes which were so like her daughter's.

'Let me make love to you, Eleanor.'

When she nodded he took her up into his arms, striding towards a door at the far end of the chamber and opening it.

His room was filled with blueness, the same wallpaper as before with its patterned cut flock. The bed was a different one, however, the coverlet now a patched quilt of mismatched fabrics.

It was here he placed her before crouching down at her feet so that their heads were level.

'This time it is your choice, Eleanor, and I need you to be sure...'

'I want you.' She gave him her answer without thought because she did. She was certain in a way she had never been before.

'And if I never retrieve my memory?'

'Then we will make new ones. Together.'

'Starting now?'

She reached out to run her hand across his cheek, the skin rough beneath the pads of her fingers. 'I wish I had been there for you when this happened.'

'And I thank the God above that you were not.'

Tipping his forehead down against her own, he sucked in breath.

'I have slept with other women, Eleanor, both here and in America, and while I have not been a saint I promise from now on it will only be you in my bed. For ever. Is that enough for you? To take all the parts of me that are damaged and still want what is left?'

His voice shook and she knew the depth of all he was saying, his years of lostness marked in sorrow. And, now, honesty.

She had loved him as a boy, but she loved him twenty times more over as this man. Strong. True. Hurt. Dangerous.

Her hand dipped into her bodice and she showed him the ring that hung at the bottom of her chain.

'You gave me this one of the last times we were together and I have not taken it off since.'

The gold caught the flame in the fire and she saw the flash of it in his eyes, his pupils distending and tightened into brown as he looked away.

It was like turning a key in a lock and the door finally opening. He remembered. He remembered laughing with her as he had bought the ring from a small shop in Piccadilly after their kiss at Lackington's. It was a celebration gift to go with the wine and hamper from Fortnum and Mason.

Her blue eyes had matched the stones and she had loved them. Zircons, the man had called them. Imitation diamonds.

And with that small crack in memory other walls began to teeter and fall and it all came tumbling in, his lost days and weeks.

He cursed as his hands flew to his head because colour slammed into his temples, not quite painful, but almost. Rushing words and images and the noise of voices. And there in the very centre of everything was Eleanor, laughing, crying, lying there beneath him with love in her eyes.

'I saw you at the Vauxhall Gardens. You were with your grandmother and we met in front of the rococo Turkish tent.'

'You remember?'

'It was evening for the lights had just been turned on and you had dropped your coin purse as I passed you and I bent to pick it up.'

Her blush surprised him.

'You told me your name was Antoinette? Why?'

'I'd recognised you and yet you did not seem to know me and with all the stories that circulated about your exploits I thought I should be a more interesting acquaintance if my name was exotic.'

'You spoke with a French accent?'

'An accent and name which you knew as false in the first moment of conversation.'

He began to laugh. 'Your grandmama called to you to come back to her and you grabbed my hand and ran.'

'I was fresh out of the schoolroom and it was said by everyone in society that you were reckless and fascinating. It was my chance for an adventure and I took it.'

'Six days?'

'Pardon.'

'We were here six days later. At Bromley House in bed together.'

'Are you shocked I was so shameless?' Her teeth sat on the fullness of her bottom lip.

'No. I thank the lord that you were.' Frowning he sought for another recall. 'Ellie? I called you that, didn't I?'

'Yes.'

'And you were a virgin.' He sobered. 'And it was my fault. If you had never been at the Vauxhall Gardens you may have been spared.'

'Spared?'

'Of all that came next. It was my arrogance that led to the incident in the alley behind Vitium et Virtus. If you had not met me…'

He stopped because he could not quite say it.

You were the Duke of Westmoor's only daughter with all the possibilities in life that such a position implied. And I took that away.

He saw her swallow and find her answer. 'If I had not met you then we would not have Lucy?'

'I want you, Eleanor. I promised myself that I would go slowly and let you choose the time and the place. I told myself that I could wait and court you, do it properly this time, with good food and the finest wine and music. But I can't. I swear I can't.'

Her hands came up to both sides of his face

and she brought him in. 'Then that is a good thing, for I do not wish any more to love a ghost.'

Love? The word vibrated on the end of his tongue, in question and in relief, but the heat that lay between them was building, a desperateness that held no mind of circumstance or propriety.

He wanted to claim her as his own, keep her here in his bed so that she might never leave him. He wanted to know every part of her as well as he knew his own body.

His mouth came down across hers in a single movement, her lips opening to his own, so that he could come inside and taste. Her sweetness and her fear.

'I will not hurt you, Eleanor.' He whispered this against the alabaster of her cheek.

'I know.'

He should be careful, he should be gentle and tender, but he could be none of those things. He kissed her as though she had always been his. His. To keep and to hold.

His hands were on the long row of tiny buttons now at the back of her gown, fumbling, shaking. He could not recall a time he'd been so desperate or so clumsy.

And then the fabric gaped, exposing the

lawn below and the skin beneath. Her breasts were round and pink tipped, the stuff of dreams and hope.

'My God,' he said quietly, as she simply stood there naked to the waist, watching him. 'You are so very lovely.' One finger trailed along the fullness to the nipple and he quickened the movement to run back and forward so that it tightened into hardness. She stretched, taken unawares, and his mouth fell to the corded elegance of her throat.

She was breathing hard now, the sound of it loud in the room, as she melted into acquiescence, shivers chasing each other across her skin. Undoing the gown further, he was pleased when the yellow wool pooled at her feet and the lawn of her petticoat covered only the thin lace of her drawers.

The chill of the room came across her bareness, her skin alight with the flame of the fire and the heat inside.

He was careful as he dealt with the last of her clothes and then she was naked before him, save for the silk stockings with the garters pulled up by pink ribbons and the soft silver slippers on her feet.

'Eleanor.' He moaned this, the breath of him reaching across the small distance between them and he knew only pain as he bent to lift her into his arms, close against his chest, because if he hurt her again he would never forgive himself.

Chapter Fourteen

He was fully dressed and she wore almost nothing, yet Eleanor understood the truth of all that she had imagined. Her legs opened and his hand rested in the junction of her thighs before slipping lower, into the place that was hidden and wet with her want of him.

He looked at her without blinking, the movement of his fingers deepening and quickening, like a maestro or a magician, and she pressed back into the patched quilt and only felt. The rush of lust, the dislocation of time, the wet warmth of her and the thick need of him.

Higher and higher she went as he came on to the bed above her, his swollen manhood replacing his fingers, the smooth sheath of it penetrating deep and then deeper.

Filling up the loneliness and despair.

When he tilted her with one arm beneath

her waist her eyes flew open and she kept
him there tight with her muscles, regulating
movement, in wildness and in ecstasy. When
he changed the rhythm of it there was a loos-
ening, the spiralling lack of control sliding
over an edge into the realm where everything impossible could happen, where life
was changed into before and after, where her
whole body jolted to the beat of the music
he made. There was no question in it but
certainty, clawed together in the chant of a
melody that was eternal, a fine unbearable
pain cleaving them into another world, as she
reached for all that was offered.

She felt the waves of release and rode them,
on and on into the nothingness and the light,
her heart beating along with his, their breath
melded in the heat. Bound by something neither of them could forget.

Afterwards they lay together on the bed
and listened to the crackle of the fire and the
wind at the shutters and the rain on the glass.
Her head was tucked into his shoulders and
his arm lay heavy across her, the smell of sex
and sweat in the air and exhilaration, too, a
memory that had not been faulty, a known
pleasure that filled her heart with joy.

'It was just like the last time…?'

His half-question was filled with such awe it made her heart's blood sing.

Her reply held the same wonder. 'Almost, but even better.'

The counterpane was across them now, the stitchery rough and frayed. Like their lives, patched from bits, making a new whole pattern from all the pieces of what had been.

She smiled and his eyebrows raised up.

'What are you thinking?'

'I was wondering where this quilt came from.'

'Remember I told you of the reverend in Boston?' He waited until she nodded. 'His wife made this for me and it represented hope for a long while after. But now…' His voice tailed off into the silence and he began again. 'Now my hope is here with you.'

He pulled her across him, his bare chest tickling her. He had removed her stockings and the remainder of his own clothes after they had made love and settled her against him so that they might understand more of each other in the closeness.

'If you had not returned, Nicholas…'

He stopped her. 'I am here and I shall never go again.'

'You promise?'

He lifted his hand and removed his signet ring, the gold of it heavy in the light.

'For you, my love, in troth.' He fitted it across her thumb and the crest of the Bromleys was easily seen in the fire flame. She covered the piece with her other hand so that it was tucked into warmth.

But the magic had seeped in again between them, the enchantment and the need as he sat her above him and came into her centre, without warning, watching her all the time.

'I like looking at you when you are breathless and I like the way your hair hangs like a curtain hiding us from the world.'

'Can we stay here for ever? Just the two of us? Like this.'

He'd begun to push in further, lifting her with the movement, her knees on each side of him steadying balance and his hand tightening around one breast.

'Come with me, sweetheart. Come with me to the edge of reason and beyond.'

She laughed at that, though the sound was not simple. Rather it was layered with lust and passion and desire.

Later she awoke to hear bells pealing out the hour of three, soft in the winds of winter.

Nicholas was not in the bed. He was sitting at the window with a blanket about his nakedness and his long hair loose, one curtain drawn back so that he might look out into the night.

A fierce night, she thought, with the raindrops hitting hard against glass and the stripped branches of bare-leaved trees swaying in the force of breeze.

The fire was banked now, only embers, small flares of occasional orange banishing back darkness. Suddenly she was afraid for them both, unreasonably and forcibly.

As if he knew what she was feeling, he turned, the scar on his cheek in the moonlight raised in a relief so that the shadow of the wound enveloped the whole of one side of his face.

He had remembered other things in the night as he sat at the window, darker things and less ordered. He recalled feeling full of shame and regret the first time they had made love because he knew that he was not worthy of Eleanor and yet he had taken her virginity without a backward glance. She made him hopeful and foolish for things that might never come to pass, good things, proper things in a lifetime that had been remarkably dissolute and disordered.

Once he'd had nothing much to forfeit, but now…

'If I ever lost you again, Eleanor…' He stopped, unable to carry on. He did not hold back his honesty though he wished there was more warmth to his words instead of a bleakness, empty of belonging, devoid of hope.

He had never had someone stay in his life. Not since his mother had kissed him goodbye and told him she would be home before he knew it, the mis-truth in her words still there in his mind. Love did not conquer fear at all, it amplified it and made it stronger, the loss a hundred thousand times worse because the promise had sounded so very sweet.

Eleanor had risen, the quilt draped about her. 'You won't. You won't lose me again.'

His heart was beating so fast at her words he wondered if she might hear it and when she came against him he opened the blanket and she sat upon his knee, all warmth and softness and violets. He pulled the quilt tightly in about her, banishing any drafts. She felt the tension in him, rippling through his body.

'You are cold?'

'No, not cold, but fearful.'

'For us?' she questioned and he nodded, because her confession of love was still ringing in his blood.

'If anything happens to you because of me…'

Her hands came around him, sealing off the loneliness. He felt a finger reach out and take his nipple in a hard grasp and with a start he leaned back.

'I liked it when you did this. Is it the same with you?'

Her other finger flicked the opposite nipple and it was suddenly harder to concentrate on the yawning desolation inside him.

'If we have only now, Nicholas, we should use it wisely.'

There was a tone in her voice he had never heard there before, the tone of a courtesan, perhaps, who knew that even a moment of pleasure took care of every other doubt.

'Wisely?'

Her hand trailed downwards and she cradled his growing hardness between her fingers.

'You are ready and so am I.'

'For an untutored lover, Eleanor, you are surprisingly bold.'

'When you have society's very best teacher, is there any wonder to it?'

He laughed then and the sadness was pushed back further, quick desire left in its place.

'This time let me show you another way of loving.' He removed the quilt and the blanket and stood her before him, kneeling in front of her and parting her thighs, pleased as the skin he could see rose up into goosebumps of delight.

She could not believe such a thing was possible, his lips against her femininity and his tongue penetrating the place between her legs.

She'd wanted to give him comfort and instead… Every thought flew from her mind as other feelings began to build and her hands moved down to hold him there.

'Don't stop.' Her voice was harsh as she opened to him further. 'Don't ever stop.'

She was wicked and wanton and shameless as she called his name and rose again over the top of pleasure and into the realms of the gods Eros and Aphrodite, their voices calling only for her.

When it was finished he stood, his mouth coming over her own and she tasted herself on his tongue and liked it. Musky. Salty.

Sweet. All the hues of desire and wanting and needing.

'Love me, Nicholas. Love me for ever.'

'I do, Eleanor. And I will.'

She was dressed when he awoke next and she insisted on going home alone before the dawn broke properly and London awoke into a new day.

'Lucy will know I am missing if I stay and I don't want her to think…'

'Her mother has spent the night loving her father?' His question broke over her words, but there was a warm note of teasing in his voice. 'Meet me again tonight. Here.'

When she nodded it was as if everything in his world was right and he kissed her, softly this time and with intent.

'Don't come down with me, Nicholas. Let me remember you here, warm from sleep and naked.'

Without his clothes on he could do nothing but watch her open the door.

'You asked for the Westmoor carriage to come back for you at this hour?'

'I did.'

He smiled because the arrangement was so much like her, unusual and different.

'Tell your brother I will call on him at one o'clock in the afternoon.'

She nodded and then she was gone.

The note came to the Bromley town house at nine-thirty in the morning and was delivered by Browne.

'This came especially by one of the Duke of Westmoor's servants, my lord. The message accompanying it stressed the fact that the Duke thought it might be important and you were to be made aware of it immediately.'

'Thank you.'

When Nicholas looked at the writing on the missive he knew a momentary failing of hope. The same hand as the spymaster in the docklands. A new lead. Another pressing difficulty.

Meet me at noon. I have some new information that will interest you. Come alone.

The game had begun again then, he thought. It was just as it always had been in the Americas. Let your guard down for a moment and the demons would pounce.

They had in Boston and in Philadelphia and

in Richmond. They had here in London, too, after the New Year's dinner at Jacob's when his carriage had been attacked.

Had someone been watching the house? Could they have seen Eleanor leave? Had they been observing him as he had visited Gunter's and Lackington's and the Bullock's Museum with her at his side, laughing, listening.

Could they learn about Lucy, too? An innocent five-year-old child whose only crime was that she was his daughter.

The world began to spin and Nick sat down, trying with all his might to remember what had happened after he had been hit on the head in the alley behind Vitium et Virtus for any clue that might aid him. He'd already ruled out his uncle's involvement, but having his full memory return was of utmost importance to Nick. If he could remember this part of his past then it might unlock other memories.

Two men had been waiting, crouched in the bushes just in the place his ring was found. They'd said something of collecting a gambling debt, he remembered that, as they had bashed him across his head. He had gone down heavily before getting up again to try to fight his way out of it. But the dizziness had been all consuming and although he managed a few more punches it had not been long until those who wanted him hurt had got the upper hand.

He remembered the moment he had twisted his ring off and thrown it into the bushes, a slow motioned arc that was then cut short by another heavy thud of wood over his head.

Then all he knew was water and running and the shout of voices, the dark of night and a boat turning on an outward tide, a gangplank, a ship's captain who took him to a small dank cabin and left him there.

All these thoughts turned in the chaos.

He had run himself, away from a life he could no longer fathom, reasoning that safety lay in the need for flight.

Instinctive. Elemental. Spontaneous.

The deep chasm of his life flowed in again, the danger, the shadows, the people who had been hurt in the Americas only because they knew him.

The ringmaster was already there this time even as some church bells chimed twelve. There were two ales on the table and beside him a thin dark man sat.

'Tell him,' the older man instructed the

stranger as Nick also took his seat. 'Tell him what you told me and don't you leave nothing out, mind.'

The man paled and cleared his throat, his voice shaky and nervous as he started into the tale. 'It is said that there is a new mark out on Viscount Bromley and the bagging of the prize is rich. A hundred pound for those who can take him.'

Nicholas's blood had frozen at his name, but in company such as this it did not pay to give too much away.

'He is a toff. He was the one who they had followed to America, only this time he's here in London and there is no need to cross the ocean to kill him.'

'Who gave the orders?'

'The secret man. No one has seen him, but the gold he deals with is real.'

'And why are you telling me this?' Nicholas stressed the personal pronoun with a flourish.

''Cos it is said that your pay is almost as good and a lot less dangerous, guv. My wife insists that I have to abide by the law from now on if I am to be any use to her, but if I can pick up a bob here or there on the way, well, whose to know the difference?'

'Have you heard anything of a plan?'

'It's a snatch from what I hear, at night. Maybe at his town house or the place of his lovebird.'

'Lovebird?'

'That was mentioned in the note. A woman who is a lady.'

Nicholas schooled his fury and his absolute and utter shock. All he showed was the interest a thief-taker might, distant and unattached as he dug into his pocket and handed over twenty pieces of gold.

He did not hedge his bets this time. No, this time he revealed his hand in all its rich glory. Let there be no question as to whether or not he would reward well for more information along the same lines.

The ringmaster gathered the coins, allowing the thin man one third of the pieces and himself the rest. The art of intelligence was never cheap or easy, every pimp knew that.

'Find me a name and you will be able to leave London and buy land for yourself on the reward. I promise it.'

Both men now looked at him, their jaws slack and their eyes wide, and it was he who left the room first this time, the tavern-keeper tipping his head to him as he left.

He could not visit Eleanor again. He could

not be seen with her. He had to stay his distance to keep her and their daughter safe, whatever the cost.

The well-spoken lord with the gold was watching him. Watching them. Only in cunning could he outwit the fellow, but he had to start his campaign right now. This minute.

The gall stuck in his throat as he understood exactly what he must do.

Three hours after Nicholas was supposed to have been there he sent a note. Even her brother looked worried at the missive.

'If Nick is hurt, it will serve him right for not asking any of us to help him.'

But the world had begun to fade for Eleanor, the tunnel of light darkening as she read the words, scrawled in his upright hand with black ink on white paper.

I am sorry. I can't. Forgive me.

It was happening again, only this time he was doing it himself, without excuse.

She tried to grab at the chair beside her but the world had shrunk and with only the barest of sighs she sank down into the oblivion that was claiming her.

She came awake with both Jacob and Rose kneeling around her, their faces full of shock and disbelief.

'If this means what I think it does, I am going to damned well knock Bartlett's head right off his shoulders.' Her brother's voice was harsh and Rose was trying to calm him, but her other hand was shaking as she sought Eleanor's.

'There must be a mistake.'

'No mistake. I know Nick's writing and it is his hand.' Jacob roared this out.

'Did you have an argument?' Her sister-in-law's words were whispered, almost un-hearable.

'An argument?' Eleanor could not under-stand what she meant.

'For Viscount Bromley to break it off like this and after you returned in the early hours this morning?'

Shaking her head, Eleanor swallowed, a retch of sickness threatening at the back of her throat.

She could not believe it. She had let herself trust Nicholas Bartlett only to be abandoned summarily and completely and left to deal with the consequences all over again.

My God, how foolish could she be? How gullible? How very duped?

And yet even now, lying here with the smelling salts under her nose and sweat upon her brow, she could not understand how it was all a lie. And that was the worst of it. Her belief in him. Her never-ending absolution, the mercy of the damned.

She felt both broken and repaired even as she thought it, her own heart hardening around the softness she had admitted to him, relegating it to a lesser place, resolve filling in around the cracks.

It was over this time. She would never trust him again and she was only glad he had not become better acquainted with Lucy and that the secret between them would not now impact on the very happiness of their daughter.

'Don't hurt him, Jacob.' She took his hand and held it close. 'You have to promise me you will not hurt him.'

Much later she crept into the room of her sleeping child and sat on the chair beside the bed, simply watching her breathe. They had been on their own for years and survived, just the two of them. They had not needed another to make their lives whole and good and they

most certainly did not need Nicholas's inter-
ference confusing matters.

They would survive.

As she pulled the blankets back into place
over the sleeping form, Lucy's eyes opened,
looking straight at her in that particular place
that lies between sleep and wakefulness.

'I love you, Mama, for ever and ever.'

'Till a million years,' Eleanor said back in
the way they had done ever since she could
recall.

'And then one more,' Lucy returned, the
smile on her face fading as her eyes closed.

Always one more, Eleanor thought. Eternity and one more. One more chance. One
more night in his bed. One more betrayal. The
tears that she had been holding on to all evening fell then in wet runnels down her cheeks
and she simply sat in the light of the banked
fire and did nothing at all to stop them.

Chapter Fifteen

Rose came in as Eleanor was eating lunch the next day and she was bristling with news that she wanted to share.

'Oliver is to be married tomorrow afternoon to Cecilia Lockhart at Vitium et Virtus. The ceremony will be performed under a special licence and we are all invited.'

'All?'

'Jacob and I. Frederick and Georgiana. Nicholas Bartlett and you. Jacob has promised to behave himself, but I am not certain what may happen when he sees Nicholas.'

Eleanor's heart sank. 'No. I won't go. Not yet.' The words fell out in a whisper.

'And you think that is wise?'

'Pardon?'

'To refuse to attend when the people you hurt by such an absence had nothing at all to do with any of it? Cecilia specifically asked for you to be there.'

'I barely know her.'

'She likes you. She admires your fortitude. She has told me this over and over again. The wedding is a small one and if you do not come people might also wonder why and any gossip can be damaging.'

'I cannot see him, Rose. I just cannot.'

'There are always two sides to every story, Eleanor. What if Nicholas Bartlett is scared of commitment because he is running from something we cannot even begin to comprehend? There are so many questions about Lord Bromley. His disappearance. His scars. His hurt and his danger.'

Eleanor shook her head. 'But he will not let me help him, Rose. I get closer and then he moves away.'

'Which is exactly what happened between Jacob and I. Should I have just given up on your brother when I was let go from the household? Should I have left my heart there at his feet to never see him again and gone to hide in shame and sadness all on a mistake? If I had, where would I be now?'

Eleanor smiled, for she could see exactly where Rose was going with this.

'You think I should fight for him?'

'I do. Because a man who is worth such emotion is also the one who could keep your broken heart safe.'

'And if it does not work out?'

'Then you will have done what you could and will have no regrets whatsoever. It's a tiny wedding. The only guests there are our friends. It will be the easiest place to see Nicholas Bartlett again with all the celebrations going on about you.'

'If I agree, I need to be able to leave when I want to. I am not staying if...'

She did not go on and was glad when Rose nodded at her condition.

She saw him the first moment she came into the main room of the club. He was standing with Frederick Challenger and Oliver Gregory in one corner, dressed in dark blue and beige, the tan of his face made deeper by the whiteness of his neckcloth.

The last time she had seen him he had been naked in bed, flushed by the exertion of sex. Almost as if he could hear her thoughts he looked up, eyes unreadable and a new stiffness in the set of his shoulders and head.

Her brother beside her swore underneath

his breath and she understood at that moment this occasion was every bit as difficult for him as it was for her. The undercurrents of friendship, betrayal and enforced joviality hung over Jacob's face as she stole a glance at him, the sort of emotions that were probably as clearly visible on her own.

Cecilia was laughing on the other side of the room with Georgiana Challenger and as they went over to join them she saw Jacob carry on stiffly towards the men.

She felt like the bad apple who had brought the rot into a barrel, distance amongst good friends, uncertainty to a group who had managed thus far to triumph over every adversity sent their way.

Nicholas had not even once caught her glance and her brother's stance was sure to be noticed by Frederick and Oliver.

Shaking her head at self-blame, she refused to harbour such nonsense. It was not she after all who had taken what was offered and thrown it all away.

'Thank you for being here, Eleanor.' Cecilia took her hand and held it. 'I only wanted a very small wedding, but I was adamant that it should include women who might be to me like Jacob, Fred and Nicholas have been to

Oliver and I have always admired the way you have lived your life exactly in the way you might want it.'

Such words were so unexpectedly sweet, Eleanor simply nodded. Cecilia Lockhart had had her detractors, but she had not ever let them sway them from her cause. Her life had not always been easy, either, for the gossip was rife when any beautiful and mysterious newcomer graced the hallowed halls of the *ton*.

'I am very honoured to be asked today, Cecilia. Oliver has been a fixture in the life of the Huntingdons for a long time now.'

The compliment, however, did make her braver and she was glad for the light pink gown she had donned which suited both her figure and her colouring and was one of her favourite dresses. Her hair had been fashioned with only the minimum of fuss and, in an embroidered half-cape to keep out the cold, she knew she looked her best which was important to her today.

A woman with a thousand other pathways to choose. Boudica, the warrior of the Iceni tribe, Ethelfleda, Queen of Mercia, or Gwenllian Gruffydd of Wales. Strength filled Eleanor where doubt had otherwise lingered and she lifted her chin. The power of womanhood could shine as brightly in adversity as it ever did in triumph.

As Frederick called for them all to gather closer and a minister she had not noticed before took his place, she made her way to the large windows at one end of the room. A bower of paper roses had been placed there with streams of cream ribbon and green holly. Appropriate and beautiful for a New Year wedding in a venue that had been important to both Cecilia and Oliver.

Of a sudden her own worries were pushed aside and she felt the delight of a couple who were well suited and about to be joined in holy matrimony.

Nicholas was the best man. This fact surprised her as he came to stand next to Oliver, a ring box in hand. Frederick and Jacob were right next to him, a group of four men who had been close friends since childhood. Each had a sprig of winter jasmine in their lapel and there was a large vase of the same perfumed flower on a table behind the bower. Jacob still looked out of sorts, but less so than he had done on first entering the club. Perhaps he had had a word with Nicholas? She hoped so.

'We are gathered here today for the marriage of…'

The words of the minister sounded out over silence and it was then that Nicholas Bartlett truly looked at her, his velvet brown eyes locking into her own with a sort of pained desperation.

Shock tore down Eleanor's spine, for everything she could see on his face was the exact opposite of the words that had been in the note.

She could not take her eyes from his and for a good ten seconds they looked into each other's souls and then away. Her heart was beating so fast and hard she felt slightly sick.

Disorientated. Dizzy. Gritting her teeth together, she concentrated on the wedding.

Cecilia looked radiant and Oliver looked… She could not quite describe how he looked. He was a very handsome man who had set the *ton* on fire with his charm and grace, but he had never seemed quite relaxed. Today he did, his smile wide and his eyes bright with love. Their hands were joined tightly together, the white of his knuckles easily seen from where she stood.

They were perfect.

And, God, she wanted that for herself, the

melding of one person to the other so that the whole was better than the two halves.

Swallowing twice, she tried to catch on to a failing fortitude. She had known such perfection as she had lain in the heat of Nicholas's bed and loved him.

Her cheeks burned as the minister glanced her way and then the rings were exchanged, Cecilia's a small white-gold circle with diamonds and Oliver's a wider plain gold band.

Nicholas looked thankful that this part of the service was over. Would he make a speech?

She heard Rose sigh beside her and looked at her sister-in-law who was dabbing her brimming eyes.

'Weddings always make me cry,' she explained. 'It's the hope in them, I think, and the promise.'

Her own lack of true participation made her feel guilty. She had been so preoccupied with seeing what Nicholas looked like up there that she had hardly spared a thought for either the bride or the groom. When she was called up to the front to sign the marriage papers as a witness she was shocked for she would have to stand right next to Nicholas Bartlett and look him in the eye whilst acting as if she was neither devastated nor heartbroken.

The pretence of it was almost too much to bear.

Rose's elbow came against her, urging movement, and smiling, even though it was the last thing she wished to do, she stepped forward.

Nicholas Henry Stewart Bartlett. He was left handed. She had not known that, but he used his damaged arm to sign his name, with the bandage just visible under the dark cuff of his jacket.

And when he had finished he turned and gave her the pen, his fingers touching hers at the transfer.

'You need to place your name beneath mine.' Today the accent of the Americas could be heard squarely in his words. A further separation. Another distance.

With care she bent to add her name to the document, although all she could concentrate on was the feel of him at her side.

He had never said 'I love you' when she had been in his bed at the Bromley town house. In the throes of desire and lust he had promised her a lot less than she had promised him and yet he had not been dishonest. He had asked for her consent and she had given it. But he had never spoken of his love.

Now as he stood next to her speaking with Jacob and Frederick and with six inches between them, all she wanted to do was to move closer and touch him.

Eleanor had barely looked at him save for one glance just before the ceremony began. She was smiling at Cecilia now, a smile that gave the impression that every single thing in her world was exactly as she would want it, his defection a trifling thing, a small inconvenience only.

Eleanor's middle name was Christine. Like her mother's. Like their daughter's.

Eleanor Christine Elise Huntingdon. He consigned her full name to memory.

He was glad that Jacob and Frederick and Oliver were here. It made the day safer somehow with them around. Eleanor would also accompany her brother and sister-in-law home afterwards. A further protection. For the next twelve hours he would not need to worry about her at all.

The thought of that made him smile and as he turned he caught her eye. She smiled back. And the world simply stopped. Just her and him in a room full of winter sunlight and flowers.

The ache of sorrow inside him nearly brought him to his knees, there in the blue salon of Vitium et Virtus, for after the joy of Oliver's happiness his own seemed compromised beyond recognition and there was nothing now that he could do to make it different if she was to stay safe.

I will always love you.

God, had he just said that? Relief filled him when he realised the words were in his head, although Jacob was looking at him oddly, a sort of shared understanding in his eyes that made no sense whatsoever.

He was pleased when Frederick called him away to help with the wine that had to be brought up from below because it allowed him an excuse to leave her side and regain his sense.

Once in the cellar Frederick turned on him. 'What the hell are you doing, Nick? Eleanor looks as though you have just stabbed her through the very heart and Jacob has all the appearance of a man who wants to kill you.'

'My memory is back, Fred, and Eleanor Huntingdon and I were close once.'

'How close is close?'

'We were together just before I disappeared.'

'God,' he said as his hand slid through his hair, sweeping it back. Such blasphemy in a man usually so very articulate worried Nick further.

'And now? It's Oliver's wedding, for God's sake. Even he is starting to realise that things are not quite right.'

'Someone wants to do her harm, Frederick, because of me.'

His friend put down the bottles he had gathered and took in a deep breath. 'Another note?'

He shook his head. 'A meeting this time. The informant told me Eleanor was being watched.'

'So you think to put distance between you. To fool the one who wants to harm you?'

'If it looks as though I am interested in others I think he will only target me. With my history…'

Fred swore again and took the cork from a bottle of wine before finding two glasses and handing him one. 'I think we need this more than anyone above does.'

There was silence for a moment before Nick began to speak.

'I'm the father of her child, Fred. We slept

together again two nights ago and the next day I discovered that she was a target, too, because of it. If anything happens to her...' He could not go on.

'You love her? My God, you do.' A smile covered his friend's face, broad and surprised. 'You never do things by half, Nick, I had forgotten that about you. You couldn't just tell her?'

'That someone still wants to kill me and that if she's in the way she will be hurt, too? She'd never let me out of her sight.'

'I see your point, for Georgiana would be exactly the same. Jacob has to know, though, so that he can make sure Eleanor stays safe when in his care.'

'You're right.'

'And Oliver is part of it, too.'

'Tell them today for me after I have left, Fred, when you think the time is right.'

'And what will you do?'

'Keep looking for some clue as to who it is who hates me so much and then deal with him.'

Nicholas raised his glass, calling the small crowd before him to order, and Eleanor turned to listen. She had not spoken to him again after the signing of their names as witnesses, but instead looked about the room, seeing the club through the eyes of someone who had never been in this type of place before.

She'd been astonished by the large array of books on the shelves and if the statues and pictures were more than racy, then that, too, added to the character.

Nicholas looked at home here, she thought, the stuffy strictures of the *ton* disappearing completely and there was a freedom inherent in the place that was beguiling.

Cecilia and Oliver were now standing next to him and he smiled at each of them before beginning to speak.

'I've had no true experience with marriage and what it entails, but it seems that love conquers all difficulties and any problems. It moves people on from one place to a better one where together they can solve life's problems. It makes them stronger, more whole, more accepting, bolder. So here's to adventure and courage and to faith in the future. Here's to Cecilia and Oliver Gregory. To a long life together and a happy one.'

Faith in the future? He'd used those same words before they had slept together and look where they had got her. The wine tasted like dry vinegar in her mouth as she raised her glass along with the others. Another few moments and she would be able to slip away from such lies and go home to Lucy. Tomorrow she would make her preparations for returning to Millbrook. Away from Nicholas. Away from heartbreak.

'They look so good together, don't they?' Rose's words came through a tunnel and she nodded. 'Bromley, however, looks like a brick has hit him, though. He keeps glancing your way when he is sure you are not looking.'

'Guilt, I suppose.' She ground the words out quietly even as Rose laughed.

'His words on marriage are surprising for a man so frightened of commitment. Your brother looks less angered by him, too. I wonder if they have spoken?'

Without giving a reply, Eleanor tipped up the glass with the rest of her wine and finished the lot.

Chapter Sixteen

❧⟡❧

He needed to be seen. He needed to be available. He needed to wait until they pounced and then… He would deal with them as easily as he had the others in the Americas who had threatened him.

He was no longer the man that they thought him and he would use this to his advantage.

Every light was on in his town house and he had given most of the servants the night off. To set the scene and make certain that whoever watched the house was also made aware of the chance to strike.

Yesterday he had squired a dozen ladies along the pathways of Hyde Park, making sure to appear animated and entertained. Last night he had done the same at the Fielders' party, chatting to this woman and then that one, giving an impression of being most available and distinctly single. The effort of it all had exhausted him. Even this morning in town he had stopped to speak with the small groups of acquaintances he met, garnering invite after invite to all the celebrations of the *ton*.

He had not caught any sight at all of Eleanor Huntingdon and for that he was glad. Priming his duelling pistol, he slipped his knife down into the leather holder of his boot and took in a breath.

The soft London Lord was long gone. He had killed before and would do again to protect his own. It was both simple and sad because to admit to being such a menace without missing a heartbeat put him in a place that was neither honourable nor decent.

After this he could not go back and live as he had once imagined he might. If he ended a man's life here tonight, he would be outcast for ever. But Eleanor and Lucy would be safe. That thought overrode every other one.

A movement on the street caught his attention and then Frederick Challenger was there at his door, dressed in black from head to foot. He looked nothing like the second son of an earl and all of the soldier.

'I have come to help you, Nick.' His eyes

took in the gun on the table primed and ready. 'It will be here?'

'From what I suspect, yes.'

Another noise out at the front garnered their attention to the doorway, the knock surprising them. This time it was Oliver, dressed in the same sort of fashion as Frederick.

'You shouldn't be here. You have just been married.'

'Let's sort this out first, Nick. It would be hard to enjoy being away on a bridal tour knowing you were battling for your life in London and Cecilia agrees with me. Jake is out the front, too, watching for any movement.'

Nicholas could only stare at Oliver and Frederick in wonder. He was no longer alone. It wasn't just he who had to deal with this peril now. There was a chance for him to still survive and live.

An hour later Jacob came inside, too, though he barely looked at Nick, the tension between them palpable.

'Eleanor is in danger because of me, Jake, it's why I sent the note. I need to see her safe. If she is hurt in any way at all...' He didn't continue.

'You could not tell her of your plan?'

'Would you have told Rose?'

'So you thought to take this on alone without telling any of us a word about it? Would you be there if we were in trouble, Nick?'

'Of course.'

'Then I rest my case. But I warn you, at the end of all this, if you don't damned well marry my sister I will kill you myself.'

'Agreed.'

'No more lies, Nick, for it's killing us all. This time we face it together and end it.'

By the morning they doubted anyone at all was coming. Perhaps they had been warned off by the appearance of the others or perhaps the heavy rain had persuaded them to wait for another night, a better chance.

Whatever the reason they locked the front door and drew the curtains, stoking the fire into a life it had not enjoyed before and sitting down near it to feel the warmth.

'This reminds me of the time the Night Watch came to the club to question us about that girl they had found by the river who had been killed. We had a roaring fire when they knocked and it was a filthy night which was odd for the start of September.'

Oliver said this as he picked at the bread, cheese and pickles Nicholas had had brought up from the kitchens. It was the first Nicholas had heard of the murder and he wondered out aloud just why the Watch would come to Vitium et Virtus to question its owners.

'The girl was a maid who had worked for us. She disappeared a few weeks after she quit the job and moved in with a new lover.'

'Did the lover kill her?' Nick's attention was caught by the story.

'No, he was absolved because he had been drinking at a tavern close by and her body was found miles away down by the Isle of Dogs.'

Jacob continued with the recount now. 'You might have known the girl, Nick, for it was the month after you disappeared that this all happened. She was slight and dark and from the country. Cornwall, I think. Sally was her name. The strange thing was the way she had been murdered. There were rows of distinct cuts all over her body, cuts that were precisely placed in every sensual zone. She'd bled to death, it was determined, and the constables named it as a sexual crime. They wondered if there was anyone at Vitium et Virtus who might have known her well enough to want her dead, though they never caught the perpetrator.'

'My God.' Nicholas stood now, his whole body shocked by such a revelation. 'I know who did it. It was Bowles who killed her.'

'Nash Bowles?' The others looked at him as though he had just lost his mind.

'I had found him doing exactly the same thing to exactly the same girl a week before I lost my memory. He said he had paid her handsomely for such a service even as I threw him out of the club by the scruff of his neck. He had a little knife in his hand and there was a look on his face that was…deranged is the closest I can come to naming it. I didn't have the time to tell you all of it before I was taken.'

No one spoke for a second as they tried to understand the sense of it all.

'It's why he wants you dead, then. This secret.' Oliver said this, the truth of his words undeniable. 'He figured out you could put it together like you just have and identify him. When you arrived home here again every part of his life was compromised.'

'It was only a matter of time and he knew it. That is why he had your carriage attacked.' Jacob stood and hit his hand hard against the mantel. 'The bastard. I never liked him. Where the hell does he live now?'

'We'd have to go to the club and get the files,' Fred said. 'I heard he had moved earlier last year, but he was still somewhere here in the city.'

Within a second they were all ready to leave, jackets and hats on and each of them bristling with anger.

Eleanor needed to get out even for an hour, her chamber squeezing in on her with all its memories and spilled tears. Lucy was tired, too, a broken night's sleep leaving her irritable. Jacob had not come home at all, she found that out as she'd met Rose at breakfast, her face tense and strained by the fact.

'Where did he go?' Eleanor asked the question, a growing alarm building.

'He just said out. When I questioned him he told me to go to sleep and he would be back by dawn. He wasn't.'

'My God, if this has anything at all to do with Nicholas…'

'I would say it has everything to do with him, Ellie. The note. Your sadness. Jacob's friendship with a man who has betrayed you.

He was gone most of the afternoon yesterday, too.'

'I will visit Nicholas Bartlett.'

'Do you think that wise?'

'I don't know any more but to just sit here…?'

'Take Lucy for a walk in the park first to get rid of some of your energy. After that either Jacob will be home and be able to tell you the news himself or you can go to Bartlett, but in a better frame of mind.'

The plan sounded like a good one and Ellie went upstairs to find her warm cloak hat and gloves before calling for her daughter to do exactly the same.

Half an hour later she did feel better. The rain had held off and the wind had lessened and although she was cold she was also less wound up.

'Will we go home soon, Mama? Back to Millbrook House?'

'I am not certain, sweetheart. There are a few things here in London still left for me to do.'

'Is Papa one of those things?'

She stopped and looked at her daughter. 'Why do you ask that, Lucy?'

'Because you have seemed sad and lonely and you said I would see Papa soon. I wish I could.' Lucy was holding her hand as they walked to head back to their carriage when another conveyance drew up closely beside them.

'Get in,' the man inside said as the door opened and her heart hit the bottom of her stomach in a horrible jolt of surprise. She pushed Lucy behind her, fearing that the gun Nash Bowles held in his hand was about to go off.

'I will shoot twice if you do not get in, Lady Eleanor, for I have absolutely nothing left to lose. I will allow you only the one warning.'

The new address of Nash Bowles proved more elusive to find than they hoped it would be.

'I know he left town for a while a few months back for he got in trouble with a gambling debt and went into hiding somewhere in the English countryside. But when he returned, I thought we had some sort of an address for him.' Frederick was now crouched at a cupboard full of paper and rifling through it.

'Keep looking. It must be here somewhere.'

Jacob emptied another drawer on the desk and was sorting through the sheets of information carefully when a messenger arrived.

Frederick took it from the man it had been sent with and handed it over.

'It's for you, Nick.'

The missive was sealed by dark scented wax and tied with two strands of equally dark ribbon. Not recognising the handwriting, Nicholas tore it open and read the message inside.

If you want to see your lover and her daughter again, meet me on the north-west corner of Hampstead Heath before the hour is up. Come alone.

Fury consumed him, the red-hot waves of hatred that ran through him making his whole body shake.

'He has Eleanor and Lucy. He's taken her to Hampstead Heath.'

'Who has her?' Oliver asked this.

'Bowles. The note's from him.' Nick handed it across to Jacob, who swore roundly, and he could barely breathe as he strode to the door, leaving the note there in the unbelieving hands of his friends.

'Wait, Nick, we will come, too.'

But the violence and savagery had taken over completely now and he was a man who only wanted his guns in hand and a horse beneath him, the red-hot waves of intensity fuelling the savage need for vengeance.

He hailed a passing cabriole and made for the Heath, leaving the others there in his wake to do as they wished.

He would kill Nash Bowles if the man had even touched one hair on either Eleanor's or Lucy's head. If he had done more, it would be a slow death and no clemency in it. He did not have a moment to waste.

If Bowles used his little knife on an inch of her skin… He pushed that thought aside and concentrated instead on calming himself for what he needed to do to deal with one such as Bowles.

She knew Nicholas would come as soon as she sat in the carriage that was now parked on the edge of Hampstead Heath. Bowles had exited the conveyance a few moments ago, striding into the undergrowth behind them and telling her to stay absolutely still and quiet.

Lucy was finally speaking again and for

that one small normality Eleanor was eternally grateful. Her daughter had spent the entire trip from Hyde Park to Hampstead Heath cowering behind her skirts and crying, her shaking body the one moving point in an otherwise still carriage.

Nash Bowles was demented, she was sure of it, his eyes unfocused and wide. He hadn't spoken much, but he had written a note and given it to a messenger as they had pulled over at the side of the road in the city. A ransom demand, perhaps? When Nicholas received it he would be furious and he would come for them.

'Your papa will be here soon, my darling, to take us home.'

That information made her daughter stop sniffling as nothing else would.

'My papa is coming…?' Light shone from eyes that looked exactly the colour of Nicholas's.

'He is, sweetheart. He will be collecting his things and coming to get us.'

'Things?'

'His present for you.' She felt in the pocket of her skirt for the small outline of the box from Rundells. She had not wanted to give Lucy the necklace after what had happened, but now she used it as a carrot on the end of a long and difficult stick.

'Wait until you see it, for I know you will love it, darling. Let us think of all the lovely things it could possibly be.'

'A pony?' her daughter guessed. 'A princess. A new baby doll for the others I have. I need a mummy doll with twins next time.'

Outside Eleanor could see Bowles now standing beside a tree about twenty yards away. He had warned her not to pull the curtain in the carriage and not to move away from his sight in any way. If she tricked him, he had threatened to begin shooting and she would not risk a stray bullet with her daughter so close.

Make things normal, her mind shouted. Make things relatable to the everyday in Lucy's life. Avoid conflict and anger and excess. Smile. She lifted her lips into a dreadful parody of humour, feeling the stretch of her cheeks even as she wanted to scream.

Her calm manner seemed to finally be pacifying Lucy for she even yawned in tiredness and asked when they might be able to go home.

A good half an hour had passed since Bowles had sent Nicholas his note.

'He has an hour,' Bowles had said in a voice that hinted of darker things that might happen if the Viscount did not materialise.

She had thought to deny knowing Nicholas that well, but the day she had met Bowles in the park when buying chestnuts had probably done away with that lie. Instead she stayed very quiet, trying not to annoy him in any shape or form and watching for a chance to escape.

Nicholas suddenly appeared across the grass to one side of the conveyance and Eleanor moved in front of her daughter so that she would not notice the proceedings outside.

He looked furious and dangerous, but it was the menacing stillness of him that she noticed the most. Here was a man who had cheated death a number of times and instead of panicking he looked calm and certain. She searched his hands for weapons, but could not see any.

Nash Bowles met him as he came out of the shadows, a pistol in hand and a sneer across his face.

'Put the gun down.' Nicholas's voice came across the wind. 'Put the gun down and we will talk.'

Eleanor could see his glance coming over

to the carriage and he swallowed as he saw her face in the window.

'There is nothing at all to be gained here by violence, Bowles.'

The other laughed. 'In that you are wrong, Bartlett, for there is everything to be won in my case and everything to be lost in yours.'

'Let the woman and child go and deal with me. They have nothing at all to do with what is between us.'

The answer back was given with venom. 'With the Duke's sister here you will do exactly as I ask and if you don't…' He turned then and pointed the pistol straight at the carriage and all Eleanor could do was to wrap her body around her daughter in an effort to protect her.

'No.' Nick felt the tightness in his throat as he said the word, but he did not shout it. The man was crazy enough in his threats without adding any pressure to it. 'Shoot me, Bowles. I am the one you want. I am the one you had followed to the Americas, although I could never quite work out why you should do that.'

Bowles had turned back to him now, his lips tight in a sneer of fury.

'Throw down your weapon, Bromley. I

know you'll have one there somewhere. Take your jacket off and your belt, too. Do it.'

Nick complied, glad at least that Bowles's attention no longer dwelt on the carriage, though he made a point to come closer. The gun he'd kept in his belt was gone, but he had a knife strapped to his ankle. Soon he would be well in range to use it.

'Let me help you, Bowles. Put down the gun and there will be all the help that you need. I promise.'

'Liar.' The gun went off and Nick felt the bullet sear along the skin of the thigh that was already scarred. He dropped to his knees and breathed hard, willing the pain at bay as he stood again. If he lost consciousness he would be no help at all to Eleanor and Lucy.

He could hear Eleanor crying now in the carriage and prayed that she might stop. Attracting any sort of attention with a madman around was dangerous.

Bowles had another pistol in his hands now, primed and ready, the first one thrown down upon the grass, the smoke from the shot curling up into the air before him.

Nicholas cursed. He could not run at Bowles with his leg burning up in pain and he was still too far away to throw his knife with any accuracy. For the moment he thought it was better to keep him speaking.

'If you talk about what you want changed, I may be able to help.'

'Talk? Why? You never liked me, none of you did with your fancy names and your tight-knit friendship. All those years of trying to be a part of your group, of currying favour at Vitium et Virtus while you laughed behind my back. Did you think I would not know? I watched you that night you disappeared from the alley behind the club. I saw the henchman beat you over the head with the wooden baton as you fell to the ground. I followed you to the river where they threw you in and I hoped that the current would take you under, so that all breath was gone. But it didn't. When the hackney cab left you crawled out again and I saw fear there on your face where before had lain only arrogance and I laughed at the way you ran like a stray dog for the docks, the grip of hell itself wrapped around your very neck.'

'But you could not leave it there? You needed to make sure I was gone. In Boston and Philadelphia and Richmond?' Keep him talking, Nick thought, for in the distance he could see the outline of Frederick behind the trees and he knew Jacob and Oliver would be close behind.

'You had seen me, seen me with her, the foolish maid from your club, and do not pretend you fail to remember that. How was I to know she had some sort of a disease that meant the bleeding would not stop? How was that my fault? She died with your name on her lips, cursing me with all her life was worth, and I knew right then that you were a danger to me and I needed to see that you never returned to England.'

He had begun to shout louder now as he advanced upon him, the gun still in his hand but shaking, more perilous than it had been even a few seconds before.

'It's over, Bowles. Give it up. Take your punishment like a man.'

'You had everything, don't you see? You had every single thing that I never did. The friends. The women. The money. The looks. But now I will take it from you because I can.'

'Get out.' Nash Bowles shouted this to the carriage behind and when the door opened Eleanor stepped down with her hands held up, Lucy at her side. Nicholas made a point of not looking at them, all the worry and guilt wrapped about his heart.

'Very well—' Bowles's voice had become more flat now '—I will grant you one thing, Viscount Bromley. You alone can choose who I save and who I kill.'

The choice of the devil. Nicholas stood stock still and raised his hands high.

'Kill me. I am the one you want. No one knows anything about the maid from the club. Your secret dies with me.'

The agonising scream from Eleanor distracted them both and it was in this moment that Nick pounced, simply leaping at the man without any fear for himself, the gun Bowles held going off and the bullet whistling within inches from his head to slam into the wide hard bulk of the trunk of an oak.

His leg ached like hell, but he had Nash Bowles, twisting his arm up behind his back. Part of him wanted to finish the job, but he shook his head and reclaimed logic even as Frederick rushed in, grabbing the other arm as Oliver got his feet.

Jacob was with Eleanor and Lucy, his voice coming through the space between them in a soft quiet whisper. They were safe. They were safe. The words beat against Nicholas's breath in a litany, but then the tunnel of light that he'd fought off began to close around him.

Blood loss, he supposed, for he had felt this before. The rush of sound in his ears, the dizziness, the feeling that his mind was somehow disconnecting from his body and going some place entirely on its own.

Eleanor ran forward, grabbing at his hands from where he lay on the wet cold grass, the rain falling in his face.

'I...am...sorry.'

He mouthed the words rather than said them. The shaking was getting worse and he was cold, far colder than he had ever been in his life. Colder even than in the Caribou Valley in the north of Maine. It was his fault that Eleanor was here having to deal with this danger and fright, his demons clawing at the ordered and gentle world that she was a part of.

Her tears of fright washed across him, hot against all that was freezing, and he tried to lift his arm, but he could not. Then all he knew was darkness.

Chapter Seventeen

He woke to pain. He woke to memory and dreams and a half-world he could not quite decipher.

He knew he was thirsty, but he was finding it hard to speak for the shivers ran through him in a constant stream of movement. A wet warm flannel came across his brow and he closed his eyes against the feel of it.

'You are in the ducal town house, Nicholas, and you have been very sick. It is a week since the accident and we thought...' Eleanor's voice faltered and stopped.

'That... I...would...die.' Every word was difficult to get his tongue around. He felt as if he had a mouth full of cotton and so he swallowed and tried again.

'Lucy?'

'Is in her bed fast asleep and dreaming of the bravery of a father who came to save her.'

Save her? The words stuck dry in his throat. Save her from the danger he had placed them in in the first place? If he had not returned, none of this would have ever happened. He wanted to ask of Bowles, but didn't, the effort too much to muster.

'My…leg?'

'The bullet punctured an artery and you were lucky to escape with your life. Frederick had seen the same thing on the battlefields of Europe and tied his neckcloth around the top of your leg.'

'Useful…knowing a…soldier.'

She laughed at that and the sound warmed him as nothing else could have done.

'You nearly lost your life for us, Nicholas.'

'Worth…it.'

Then he closed his eyes and slept.

Next time he awoke he felt much better, more level headed, less dizzy.

Eleanor was still there by his bed, but dressed in other clothes now and the afternoon sun was coming in through the windows. How could that be? A few moments ago it had been night time. He lay perfectly still and watched her. Her eyes were closed and the pins in her hair loosened. One curl had slipped from its mooring and settled across the line of her breasts.

She was so beautiful she simply broke his heart.

As if she felt his gaze her eyes opened. Would he ever get used to the startling shade of blueness? he wondered, only to decide that it was very unlikely.

'Hello.' Her voice was soft with sleep. 'How are you feeling?'

'Better.'

'Would you like a drink?'

He nodded and she brought a glass of lemonade to his lips, her hand behind his neck to help him as he leaned forward.

'That is good.' The liquid was like ambrosia to his dried mouth though she did not let him have too much.

'The physician said that we were to offer this to you, but that I had to be careful about what you took.'

'Physician…?'

'He is retained by the Westmoors and has been earning his year's stipend over the past week.'

Nicholas wiggled his toes just to make sure that the leg was still there, that he had not had the thing amputated or cut into whilst he had been asleep, but everything seemed in order save the sharp ache the movement brought forth.

'You lost a lot of blood and there had been another injury in the same place which complicated things. But he says you should be able to start getting up after the next few days for the fever at least has gone.'

'Fever?'

'You burned with it for three days and nights.'

She had thought he would die as his temperature had soared. She imagined that a man could not last with such a sickness, the redness across his cheeks and his body building into rash.

She had been shocked by the scars he wore beneath his clothes for in the hard light of day they were far more extensive than she had thought them. Myriad injuries that crossed his back and his front, the worst of it being on the same thigh the bullet had passed through.

A history of violence written in flesh. She hated Nash Bowles with even more intensity than she had before. Sometimes she wondered just who she had become.

Were another threat to stalk Nicholas here

in his vulnerable state she would have had no compunction but to squeeze out the life from any assailant. She wondered where the kindly polite sister of a duke had disappeared to in the face of all that had happened.

'Where is… Bowles?'

'In jail and he will be for a very long time. Oliver and Frederick took him to the constabulary after they had seen to you. Jacob stayed here and waited with me for the doctor.'

'He is sick, I think…in the head.'

'He wished he was like you. He wanted to run Vitium et Virtus. He kept yelling that out all the way across the park even as they took him away.'

When Nicholas nodded Eleanor thought he looked tired and she stopped speaking. He had been distant since the shooting, with an edge of anger. Did he blame her in some way for endangering Lucy?

As his eyes closed she brushed away the tears that had pooled in her eyes and threatened to fall down across her cheeks.

It was later the next day when Nick felt well enough to haul himself into a sitting position and dangle his legs off the side of the bed. At the beginning his heart hammered against his temples, but then it subsided. Perhaps he would not stand just yet, he thought, looking at the thick bandage wrapped tightly about his thigh.

A small noise at the doorway alerted him to the fact that he had a visitor.

'Lucy?'

The child came further into the room. Not so close that she could not turn and run if she needed to, but closer than he held any right to expect.

'Are you better?' Her voice was tense. He could hear the vestige of fright from the incident at Hampstead Heath in what she said.

'Nearly.' His eyes went to the doll she carried and it had a sizeable bandage around its head.

'Did your doll get hurt, too?'

'Yes. By a speeding bullet. Mama says that for every three bullets that miss there is one that will find its mark.'

'I am glad it didn't find its mark with me, then.'

She smiled. 'But it did.'

'Not badly, at all,' he replied, liking how she watched him, taking him in, tossing up whether or not he was worth the fuss as a father. 'A leg is much better than a head or the chest to get hit in. Poor doll.'

At that she moved forward and set the doll down on his bed, removing the bandage deftly and retying it around a thin china leg.

'Now she is just like you and getting better. Did you know Mama cries a lot when you are not looking?'

The truth of the words had him taking in breath.

'I think she thought it was her fault that we were shot.'

'I don't think the fault was anyone's except the man with the gun.'

'Bowles. That was his name. Nasty Bowles.'

The words took him by surprise and he smiled. 'You have named him well.'

'And you are my papa. I have always wanted one. Everyone else has one and I never did.'

Again he smiled. Lucy had the same habit as her mother had of setting words down in a way that was unusual. He was glad of it.

'When you are better would you like to play dolls with me again? I could show you how to dress them, too, and feed them. I could even bring the dolls' house in here if you would want me to.'

'I would.'

At that she smiled, a full real smile that lit her eyes and brought out her dimples.

A woman then came to the door, her face furrowed with a frown. 'I have been looking everywhere for you, Lucy. I am sorry, Lord Bromley, I hope she has not been disturbing your rest.'

He watched as Lucy followed the woman out of the room and thought his daughter was every bit as beautiful as her mother.

He saw that she was wearing his locket around her neck.

Did you know Mama cries a lot when you are not looking?

Lucy's words sliced right through him. It was well past time to let her see exactly who he was and wasn't.

Eleanor came to see him just as the sun was setting. She had been in and out for small pieces of time, but always in the company of others, once with the doctor and then again with Jacob. The third time when she brought her grandmama to visit Nicholas wondered if she did not wish to be alone with him.

He could understand her reasoning. She had a daughter to see safe and so far all he seemed to have brought her was heartache and fear.

He had lived in the shadows for so long that he was now unfit to inhabit a better world, a brighter place. His presence in other good people's lives was a dark influence, a grimy dimness that invited in danger and jeopardy.

Jacob had been civil but distant after the incident in the park. As the head of the Westmoor family he could probably see the foolishness of closer relations with someone who was tainted irreparably by such chaos.

That evening Nicholas had insisted on wearing his own day clothes instead of the nightgown and he felt more like himself with each passing moment. Stronger. Less like an invalid for he knew he needed to be gone from here as soon as he was able.

Tonight Eleanor was dressed in a soft blue, the fabric picking up the colour of her eyes, but also the dark shadows beneath them.

'You look almost returned to normal?' her words more a question as she stood against the mantel, the candle there lighting up all the shades in her hair.

'The physician said that I should be able to go back to the Bromley town house tomorrow. At the end of the week I will go north to

Bromworth Manor and I am not certain when I shall be back.'

'I see.' A frown lingered now and she bit her lip.

'Eleanor…'

'Nicholas…'

Their words collided and she smiled shakily before she bade him to go first.

'I cannot be with you, Eleanor. If anything were to happen to you or Lucy because of me I would never forgive myself. There is no way I can foresee the future, but if the past is anything to go by, you would be well rid of me.'

'And Lucy? You are saying she should forget her papa when she has only just found him?'

'I am saying she needs to be safe. If there are more like Bowles out there then I will need to be wary and there are many others with their own reasons for seeing me gone. When we were searching for the culprit who was threatening me your brother and I made a list at Vitium et Virtus and there was more than a small amount of names there who held grudges against me. I cannot guarantee they will not come next, with their sharpened knives and loaded guns. It's who I am, don't you see? Tainted. Ruined. Perilous.'

He held his hand out as she began to speak because now that he was started he could not seem to stop.

'It's why I left after we…made love. It's why I sent the note to tell you that I couldn't and that I was sorry but… I will provide for you both financially for ever, but I think you should not tell anyone outside of the family that Lucy is my daughter. Who knows what other perils are lurking unbidden? The world is a far more dangerous place than you realise, Eleanor. Without me there might be a chance for safety. If I stay well away from you and from Lucy the gossip will die down and people might forget.'

Her eyes were full of tears as she stepped forward. 'I love you, Nicholas, and so does Lucy.' There was no hesitation in her promise.

He shook his head, hard. 'No. You can't say that.'

She kept coming closer, one hand placed across his arm now, her fingers holding on with all that she was worth. 'I have loved you since the first moment I ever really saw you at the Vauxhall Gardens and I've loved you more and more each day since.'

He swallowed and placed his thumb across her lips to stop the words from coming.

'I can only hurt you, don't you see?'

'You can hurt me by staying away, by believing that you are this person that you are not. We belong together, you and I and Lucy, and if there are challenges in the future we can meet them.'

'Sometimes I dream of blood.' His words held a flatness and a finality that made the back of his throat thicken. But he needed to say what he was, what he had been, what he had done. 'The blood of the man whose neck I broke by the James River. Just a quick twist and he was gone into the water though his eyes watched me as he went. The blood of others I have hurt, too, in fights and in arguments, with knives and glass and wood. This is who I am, Eleanor. You must have seen the marks on me in the sickbed. In each and every one of those scars lies the ghost of fury or fear or just plain ordinary temper.'

'Or the badge of honour? The bullet you took at Hampstead was in lieu of me and Lucy. You were trying to save us, Nicholas, by offering up your own life. I could see that in your face as you tried to draw Bowles away from the carriage.'

'I should have shot him through the head when I had the chance. And I did have that chance. I had seen him through the trees when I first arrived at the Heath. It would have been so very easy to skirt around and come up behind him to take a shot at close range. Instead I left you and Lucy in danger and it could have turned out so very differently.'

'No, don't you see?' Eleanor's voice was stern. 'Instead you tried to talk Bowles out of a course of action that was impossible. Even in danger you tried to help him, tried to defuse the situation so that he might come out of it alive. You are not a killer, Nicholas, and you never have been, but you have had to fight for your life, too, and there is no shame at all in that.'

Nicholas took in a breath at her words because he heard a truth in them that was undeniable and sweet.

'You are free now to live how you want. There is no one else ready to spring out and hurt you. Please, Nicholas, please believe it is possible.'

She could see the terror in his eyes, but she could also see the beginnings of something else. Hope, if she might name it, and faith.

With his limp and his scars and his left arm still in a bandage, with all the old hurts be-

neath his clothes and a belief inside himself
that he was damaged and dangerous and un-
knowable, Nicholas still looked beautiful to
her. More than that, though, he was beginning
to look as if he was realising it, too. Realising
that she knew the worst about him and was
still here, that no matter what he threw at her
she would not be shifted in her belief in him
and that the words she had given him, words
of love, could even possibly be true.

'You would want me like this, Eleanor?
After Hampstead Heath and being in all that
danger? After knowing who I am? Who I
truly was?'

'I want you for ever. I want to grow old
with you and have more children with you and
know what it is like to have years and years
in each other's company. That is what I want.'

She moved closer, only the smallest distance separating their bodies from what was
and what could be.

'If you love me, Nicholas, you will want
that, too.'

Nicholas swore and his dam suddenly
broke, she could see it in his eyes and on his
face and in the way his body enveloped her
own, his arms about her, drawing her in, his
breath in her hair as he held her against the

heavy beat of his heart. 'I love you, Eleanor, but I cannot believe I deserve you.'

'How much do you love me?' She was smiling now, the joy in him chasing away the shadows.

'With every fibre of my body, with every thought in my mind. With my heart and my breath and my soul I love you, sweetheart. And more.'

'Take me to bed again at your town house. I promise I will be gentle with all your wounds.'

When he laughed she heard the sound of freedom and she knew that a healing had begun.

'Perhaps we should be married first?'

She smiled at his question and nodded.

'Is your brother home tonight?'

'Yes. He is in his library.'

'Stay here, then. I won't be long at all. Don't move.'

He got down the stairs on the wings of elation for this time everything would be done in the correct order. This time he would not fail Eleanor as he had before. This time he wanted everything to be exactly as it should be.

Jacob was reading in his old leather armchair by the fire.

'Nicholas.'

The restraint that had been a part of their relationship since he had sent the note separating himself from Eleanor could be easily heard in his name.

'I need to ask you something, Jacob, but I also need to tell you things that you might not wish to know.'

Jacob stood and crossed to pour them both a drink, holding a glass out to Nick after he had done so and pulling another chair closer to the fire, gesturing for him to sit.

When he did so he felt at odds as to where to begin, but was pleased as the brandy fortified his resolve.

'I love your sister, Jake, and I want to marry her. I want to care for her and protect her and Lucy. I want to make certain that they are always safe.'

'And the part I might not wish to know?'

'I have killed a man, and done things in the Americas and here that I have no reason to be proud of. Bowles perhaps was a part of that, too, along with an arrogance and recklessness that came back to haunt me.'

'You have always been the most dissolute of the four of us, Nicholas, but then I always knew, too, that you had a good heart. I still do know that. Rose says you are like a plant, untended and wild, and that Eleanor with all her gardening skills will make certain that you grow in a way that is perfect.'

'I like your wife, Jake.'

'I like her, too.'

'Will you give your blessing on our marriage? I haven't asked your sister yet because this time I need to do things properly and I know Eleanor would like her family's support.'

Jacob stood as Nicholas did.

'More than a blessing, Nick. I want to be your best man. But right now you had better let me help you back upstairs to bed for you look as though you might keel over.'

It was late and the fire in the hearth was well banked.

They had been married for six hours and the ring on Eleanor's finger shone in the light of the flame, where two unmatched diamonds sat in a clasp of rose gold.

'It is the most beautiful piece of jewellery I have ever seen, my love,' she whispered, her cheeks flushed from their recent lovemaking and desire.

'The large one is for you and the smaller one is for Lucy. The two jewels of my heart.'

They were lying on his patched quilt in front of the fire, as naked as the day they were born. The bandage on his leg had been removed yesterday and she traced the thick red line on his thigh with care.

'Does it still hurt?'

'Only a little,' he returned, his fingers coming across the fullness of her breast, 'and not a bit when I touch you.'

The edges of his mouth were turned up, his hair soft around his face but his eyes held only an unsated need of her body and spoke a language that heralded no words at all.

Today in the tiny chapel in Mayfair they had sworn a troth to each other in front of their family and close friends. Tonight they were sealing the promise in flesh.

'Let me love you, sweetheart,' he whispered and she opened her legs to his touch, the wetness there attesting to his other ministrations and endless want.

He came in slowly this time, none of the desperation of the first hours apparent, but a quiet and languid joining. And he watched her with his velvet eyes and his smile, watched as she was pushed over the edge of reason on to the slippery slope of passion and down and down to the river of release.

This was love. This was life. This is what she had dreamed of in all the years of her sadness.

'Love me for ever, Nicholas,' she finally whispered when her breath was back.

'I will, my darling. I promise.'

Epilogue

Christmas Eve, 1819

The main salon at the ducal town house was
filled with Christmas.

There were stars cut in gold paper and
silk fabric scattered across the trestle tables
which were heavy with the fare of the season. Rosemary, bay, holly and laurel had been
brought inside this morning as it was unlucky
to have it displayed until Christmas Eve. A
roaring fire in the hearth warmed the room,
the crackle of the Yule log competing with
the excited chatter of Lucy, who was using
this evening to give out her own special gift
with all the aplomb that a six-year-old was
able to manage.

'This is for you, Papa,' she said and si-
dled up on to Nicholas's knee. The present

he opened was embellished with the sparkly red ribbon that Eleanor had given her the year before.

The year before.

So much had happened in a year, she thought, looking around the room at her brother and Rose, who was four months pregnant, and then at Oliver and Cecilia sitting together on the sofa by the fire. In Cecilia's arms was a baby who was the spitting image of his father right down to his light green eyes and coffee-coloured skin.

Frederick and Georgiana sat in the two leather arm chairs, a sleeping child in the bassinet at their feet. At six months old Harriet looked to be finally settled and her parents were enjoying a moment's respite, though Grandmama was watching closely for any sign of wakefulness in order that she might have a hold.

Nicholas's present was now revealed and Eleanor had to smile. Lucy had made him a painting for his library which she had framed in rainbows and kisses. The image showed the three of them at Bromworth Manor with their arms around each other. Victor was seated next to them, almost as large as they were, his pink tongue lolling.

'I shall hang this family portrait above my desk,' Nicholas was saying. 'Right where I can see it when I sit down to work.'

'You really like it, Papa?' There was a shy hopefulness in Lucy's voice. She always addressed him as Papa whenever she was able to. A vestige of five years without him, perhaps, that now translated into a need of constant ownership?

'I love it,' Nick was saying, her arms coming tightly around his neck in reply as he kissed her on the forehead.

'I want one for my library, Lucy,' Jacob said. 'Can I commission you?'

'Comm…ishin? What does that mean, Uncle Jacob?'

'It means he will pay you money for a portrait of him and Rose and the new baby when it comes. Make sure it's a goodly sum for he can certainly afford it.' Nick was smiling as he explained this and Lucy nodded.

'I think we should all have one, Lucy, of each family.' Oliver's voice was serious. 'It can become a new tradition.'

'Because the old ones are seeming more and more irrelevant?' Frederick laughed and his hand slid into Cecilia's. 'I don't think that Christian and his friends know quite what they are inheriting with their acquisition of Vitium et Virtus.'

'A monster?' Oliver smiled.

'A way of life that is fleeting,' Jacob amended, 'and yet...look what it had brought us. I wouldn't have met Rose had I not found her at the club late one night trying on one of the performer's dresses.'

Rose shook her head. 'The fabric was so beautiful I couldn't resist pretending for a moment that instead of being the maid I was a high-born lady dancing with a handsome gentleman.'

Lucy clapped her hands at the story and Rose blew her a kiss. 'Dream big, Lucy,' she said, 'just like I did.'

'Here's to Vitium et Virtus,' Oliver spoke next. 'And to the beautiful Madame Coquette who came my way because of it.' He lifted his glass to Cecilia, who smiled back at him, her brown eyes alight with tenderness.

'If you had not come to Paris on business for the club...' Her voice tailed off in worry.

'I would have met you somewhere, my love. Trust me on that.'

Frederick stood now with a toast. 'To Georgiana with her perfect but foolish plan at avoiding an arranged marriage. Vitium et

Virtus was the venue for her fall into notoriety and that in turn brought her straight to me.'

'There is a silver lining, Frederick, in every cloud of hopelessness.' Georgiana raised her own glass and drank.

That left only Nicholas to give the others his memory of meeting her at the club. Only they hadn't met there in any shape or form, his pool of blood discovered in the alley behind the day after he had disappeared.

'For me Vitium et Virtus was always about a family I never had. It was about friendship and freedom and if the place encouraged excess and recklessness then it also helped me to understand what I truly wanted my life to be like. Here's to you, Eleanor and Lucy. My jewels. My home. My family. The virtue to my vice.'

Frederick lifted his glass. 'To family then and to friendship. Christian told me as I left tonight that he hoped we enjoyed our one last party at the club. He has opened the cellar and given the entertainers the evening off. He said tomorrow they shall all be back and heaven help anyone who thought Vitium et Virtus had become proper.'

'He sounds like us, back then when we were young.' Nick laughed as he stated this.

'Well, it's in safe hands at least.' Oliver's voice held a good deal of the same humour. 'He has not paid us for all the bottles of liquor stored in the cellar after all, so we need to be sure to drink up deeply.'

'Can I come with you, Papa? Can I go to the club, too?'

'No, you may not, Lucy, until you are at least twenty years older and hopefully not even then.' Nicholas sounded like a protective father, his tone all that of a man who had never had a wild and reckless youth. 'It's bed for you in order to be up early for all the celebrations. But your mama, on the other hand, is most welcome to dance just with me until the morning.'

His eyes were bright with love, the wary distance gone now to be replaced by joy. A family man, a man of the land, a man who had discovered his place in life and in her heart.

Eleanor raised her own glass.

'Here's to the Christmases past and all those to come, for blessed is the season that makes the whole world love.'

And under her breath she thanked God for the best Christmas present she had ever received, the first fluttering of a new life quiet in her womb.

Tonight she would tell Nicholas when they were alone, tucked in their bed under the patched quilt on the second floor of the Bromley town house, a waxing Yuletide moon outside.

Breathing in, she looked over at her husband and when his glance caught hers she tipped her head and he tipped his back, a secret smile across his face.

Perhaps he already knew?

Her world was so full of promise and hope that she felt her own mother and father close.

You would have loved Nicholas, she thought, just as the Yuletide log suddenly flared.

They were watching with Ralph, she knew they were, from up above. Tonight of all nights she understood the eternity of family as she had not before as somewhere close the strains of a Christmas song could be heard on the wind.

Hark! the herald angels sing
Glory to the newborn king!
Peace on earth, and mercy mild
God and sinners reconciled

* * * * *

If you missed the first,
second and third stories in
THE SOCIETY OF
WICKED GENTLEMEN
quartet, check out

A CONVENIENT BRIDE FOR
THE SOLDIER
by Christine Merrill

AN INNOCENT MAID FOR THE DUKE
by Ann Lethbridge

A PREGNANT COURTESAN
FOR THE RAKE
by Diane Gaston

WE'RE HAVING A
MAKEOVER...

We'll still be bringing you the very
best in romance from authors you
love...all with a fabulous new look!

Look out for our stylish new logo, too

MILLS & BOON

COMING JANUARY 2018

MILLS & BOON®

HISTORICAL

AWAKEN THE ROMANCE OF THE PAST

A sneak peek at next month's titles...

In stores from 28th December 2017:

- **His Convenient Marchioness** – Elizabeth Rolls
- **Compromised by the Prince's Touch** – Bronwyn Scott
- **The Captain's Disgraced Lady** – Catherine Tinley
- **The Mistress and the Merchant** – Juliet Landon
- **Carrying the Gentleman's Secret** – Helen Dickson
- **The Prairie Doctor's Bride** – Kathryn Albright

Just can't wait?
Buy our books online before they hit the shops!
www.millsandboon.co.uk

Also available as eBooks.

MILLS & BOON®

EXCLUSIVE EXTRACT

Read on for a sneak preview of
COMPROMISED BY THE PRINCE'S TOUCH
by Bronwyn Scott
the first book in the daring and seductive series
RUSSIAN ROYALS OF KUBAN

'I am a prince who cannot return to his kingdom. I, too, must be careful with whom I associate.' Nikolay's voice was a caress, low and husky with caution. It was not caution for himself, but for her; a warning Klara realised too late.

His mouth was on hers, sealing the distance between them. He kissed like a warrior; possessive and proving, a man who would not be challenged without choosing to respond in kind.

Her mouth answered that challenge, her body thrilled to it. This was what it meant to be kissed, not like the few hasty kisses she'd experienced during her first Season out before it was clear she'd been set aside for the Duke. That should have told her something. Well-meaning gentlemen held their baser instincts in reserve, they didn't kiss as if the world was on fire. There was nothing altruistic about Prince Nikolay Baklanov when it came to seduction and he wanted her to know. As a warrior, as a lover, he took no prisoners.

Two could play that game. Her arms went about his neck, keeping him close, letting her body press against and softness of her. She let her tongue explore his mouth, her teeth nipped at his lip as she tasted him. There were things she wanted him to know as well. She was not one of his spoiled students. She would not be cowed by a stern look and a raised voice. She was not afraid of passion. Nor was she afraid to take what she wanted, even from him. She was good at showing people what she was not. It was easier than showing people what she was: a girl forced to marry, a girl who knew nothing about where she came from, a girl caught between worlds. Her hands were in his hair, dragging it free of its leather tie. She gave a little moan of satisfaction as his teeth nipped at her ear lobe.

At the sound, he swore—something in Russian she didn't need to understand to know what it meant: that their kiss had tempted him beyond comfortable boundaries. He drew back, his dark eyes obsidian-black, his voice ragged at its edges as if he'd found a certain amount of satisfaction and been reluctant to let it go. But there was only that glimpse before the words that indicated this might have only been a game played for her benefit, to show her what it meant to poke this particular dragon. 'Forgive me,' he began, 'I did not intend…'

Cold fury doused the newly stoked heat of her body. 'Yes, you did. You've had every intention of kissing me since we met.'

'Touché.'

DON'T MISS
COMPROMISED BY THE PRINCE'S TOUCH
BY BRONWYN SCOTT

Available January 2018
www.millsandboon.co.uk